KINGPIN PLANET

Borgo Press Books by JOHN RUSSELL FEARN

1,000-Year Voyage: A Science Fiction Novel * *Anjani the Mighty: A Lost Race Novel* (Anjani #2) * *Black Maria, M.A.: A Classic Crime Novel* (Black Maria #1) * *A Case for Brutus Lloyd* * *The Crimson Rambler: A Crime Novel* * *Death in Silhouette* (Black Maria #5) * *Don't Touch Me: A Crime Novel* * *Dynasty of the Small: Classic Science Fiction Stories* * *The Empty Coffins: A Mystery of Horror* * *The Fourth Door: A Mystery Novel* * *From Afar: A Science Fiction Mystery* * *Fugitive of Time: A Classic Science Fiction Novel* * *The G-Bomb: A Science Fiction Novel* * *The Genial Dinosaur* (Herbert the Dinosaur #2) * *The Gold of Akada: A Jungle Adventure Novel* (Anjani #1) * *Here and Now: A Science Fiction Novel* * *Into the Unknown: A Science Fiction Tale* * *Last Conflict: Classic Science Fiction Stories* * *Legacy from Sirius: A Classic Science Fiction Novel* * *The Man from Hell: Classic Science Fiction Stories* * *The Man Who Was Not: A Crime Novel* * *Manton's World: A Classic Science Fiction Novel* * *Moon Magic: A Novel of Romance* (as Elizabeth Rutland) * *The Murdered Schoolgirl: A Classic Crime Novel* (Black Maria #2) * *One Remained Seated: A Classic Crime Novel* (Black Maria #3) * *One Way Out: A Crime Novel* (with Philip Harbottle) * *Pattern of Murder: A Classic Crime Novel* * *Reflected Glory: A Dr. Castle Classic Crime Novel* * *Robbery Without Violence: Two Science Fiction Crime Stories* * *Rule of the Brains: Classic Science Fiction Stories* * *Shattering Glass: A Crime Novel* * *The Silvered Cage: A Scientific Murder Mystery* * *Slaves of Ijax: A Science Fiction Novel* * *Something from Mercury: Classic Science Fiction Stories* * *The Space Warp: A Science Fiction Novel* * *A Thing of the Past* (Herbert the Dinosaur #1) * *Thy Arm Alone: A Classic Crime Novel* (Black Maria #4) * *The Time Trap: A Science Fiction Novel* * *Vision Sinister: A Scientific Detective Thriller* * *Voice of the Conqueror: A Classic Science Fiction Novel* * *What Happened to Hammond? A Scientific Mystery* * *Within That Room!: A Classic Crime Novel* * *World Without Chance*

THE GOLDEN AMAZON SAGA

1. *World Beneath Ice* * 2. *Lord of Atlantis* * 3. *Triangle of Power* * 4. *The Amethyst City* * 5. *Daughter of the Amazon* * 6. *Quorne Returns* * 7. *The Central Intelligence* * 8. *The Cosmic Crusaders* * 9. *Parasite Planet* * 10. *World Out of Step* * 11. *The Shadow People* * 12. *Kingpin Planet* * 13. *World in Reverse* * 14. *Dwellers in Darkness* * 15. *World in Duplicate* * 16. *Lords of Creation* * 17. *Duel with Colossus* * 18. *Standstill Planet* * 19. *Ghost World* * 20. *Earth Divided* * 21. *Chameleon Planet* (with Philip Harbottle)

KINGPIN PLANET

THE GOLDEN AMAZON SAGA, BOOK TWELVE

JOHN RUSSELL FEARN

Edited by Philip Harbottle

THE BORGO PRESS
MMXIII

KINGPIN PLANET

FIRST BORGO PRESS EDITION

Published by Wildside Press LLC

www.wildsidebooks.com

DEDICATION

For Arthur Philip King

CONTENTS

THE GOLDEN AMAZON
by Philip Harbottle

In 1943 British writer John Russell Fearn decided to quit writing for the American pulp science fiction magazines, and to concentrate instead on books for the English market. Within a very few years he became established as a leading novelist in several genres, not only science fiction, but also mystery and detective fiction, and westerns.

His first new SF novel, *The Golden Amazon*, was published by World's Work in April 1944. In this story, a little girl of three years of age is made the subject of an idealistic scientist's illegal glandular experiments. The scientist's dream is to end world wars by creating a woman devoid of the usual lusts and frailties of mankind, who upon reaching maturity would institute a benign scientific rule. But the apparently successful experiment has a flaw: it instills into the girl a hatred for all men, and a ruthless cruelty. Her supernatural scientific gifts enable her to master atomic power, and practically leads her to destroy the world. She breaks the will and strength of men, and elevates women to positions of wealth and power. She also discovers human synthesis, and by this means she is able to escape retribution when she is eventually overthrown. She is seen to collapse and die, a victim of consuming ketabolism, echoing the memorable finale of Rider Haggard's *She*. In actuality, it was only her synthetic image, and this paved the way for the *Golden Amazon Returns*, and further sequels

Fearn sold reprint rights in the first novel to the prestigious Canadian magazine, the Toronto *Star Weekly*. The magazine carried a special Comics Supplement, the centre section of which was a 'complete novel', published in newspaper format. Aimed at a general readership, the novels were written by the top popular novelists of the day, including John Dickson Carr, Ellery Queen, and P. G. Wodehouse. They sold hundreds of thousands of copies, and the novels were syndicated to several American newspapers in the Maine and New York areas. The Amazon novels enjoyed extraordinary popularity (especially with Canadian housewives), and ran for the next sixteen years following the appearance of the first novel in the March 3, 1945 issue, ending with Fearn's sudden death in September 1960, aged only fifty-two. His final two Amazon novels appeared posthumously.

During Fearn's lifetime, only the first six novels were published in British hardcover editions from the World's Work in England, after appearing in the *Star Weekly*. This was because the publishers discontinued their entire fiction line in 1954. However, the Amazon novels continued to appear in the *Star Weekly*, eventually notching up twenty-four titles.

Fearn had resold paperback rights to the Canadian publisher Harlequin Books, but after publishing only the first three titles, they stopped publishing SF and other genre fiction to concentrate on their famous Romances line.

Meanwhile, as early as 1949, Fearn had realized that the Amazon series had the potential to run indefinitely. This presented him with a problem, however. The 'origin story' of the Golden Amazon was conceived and actually set during the Second World War. Subsequent novels were written during the war and the immediate postwar period, and projected their stories only a few decades into the future.

He very astutely realized that to keep ahead of reality, he needed to move the Amazon *further* into the future—first into the outer solar system, and thence to the stars. So with the seventh novel, he introduced a new main character, Abna of Atlantis—someone as equally intelligent, and even stronger than herself. These dynamics provided him with an *interstellar* canvas, thus ensuring that the series would remain ahead of reality.

Fearn's strategy was a great success, and the Amazon novels retained their popularity, ending only with his tragically early death in 1960. By then he had written a further twenty Amazon novels, and made prelimi-nary notes for his next (which would later be written by Fearn's biographer, Philip Harbottle).

Long after Fearn's death, his entire Amazon series

would eventually see print from the pioneering US small press Gryphon Books in limited paperback editions, and later by the Canadian Battered Silicon Dispatch Box small press in their hardcover Omnibus series.

This new Borgo Press paperback series will be the first trade edition of all twenty-one of these later novels by Fearn, beginning with the seventh novel in the original series. First published in 1949 as *Conquest of the Amazon*, I have edited it slightly as *World Beneath Ice* (The Golden Amazon Saga, Book One) so that it can be read and enjoyed by new readers who may be totally unfamiliar with what had gone before. Subsequent novels have also been slightly edited for modern readers.

The publishers hope that this new series may create many more "fans of the Amazon." Meanwhile, any reader interested in seeking out the earlier six Golden Amazon novels will find that they are readily available on the internet, and in numerous earlier paperback and hardcover editions.

* * * * * * * * * *

To date, readers can enjoy the following new Borgo Press editions:

Book One: *World Beneath Ice*

In destroying the threat of an alien invasion, the Golden Amazon had inadvertently caused a decline in the sun's heat, encasing Earth in an ice sheet that threatens to eliminate humanity. The Amazon encounters Abna, a descendant of Atlantis, stronger and even more scientifically advanced than she, and the ruler of an Atlantean colony still surviving in a protected environment on Jupiter. She refuses his offer of marriage, but agrees to form an alliance in order to restore the sun and save the Earth. One thing that Abna has not told the Amazon is that all the females of his race have been wiped out by a bacilli infection....

Book Two: *Lord of Atlantis*

A gigantic ridge of land rises from the Atlantic floor, causing massive tidal waves on either side of the ocean. Even stranger, both England and America are then assailed by an invasion of prehistoric monsters! A gigantic domed city rests on the newly risen plateau, whilst out in space an alien spacecraft orbits the Earth. Such are the mysteries and challenges facing the Golden Amazon, self-appointed governess of Earth, as she struggles to unravel the maze of mystery that was the deadly legacy of Atlantis!

Book Three: *Triangle of Power*

The marriage of Violet Ray Brant—better known as The Golden Amazon—and Abna of Atlantis should have ushered in an era of peace and scientific prosperity to the people of Earth. But an unexpected turn of events finds Abna betrayed and marooned on a satellite of Jupiter, and the Amazon flung far beyond the Solar System. With Earth's two protectors removed, the planet is now at the mercy of another Atlantean, the master scientist Sefner Quorne....

Book Four: *The Amethyst City*

The metaphysical union of the Amazon and Abna results in the mental creation of a fully mature daughter—Viona. Quorne, still struggling for domination, forces Viona into a marriage ceremony, and impregnates her. But with the intervention of Tarnec Brodix, a supermind from an external universe, Quorne and Viona are separately flung into an ultra-dimensional limbo. Abna chooses to follow after his daughter, leaving the Amazon to brood over the disaster, alone in the Amethyst City of Saturn.

Book Five: *Daughter of the Amazon*

A miscalculation by the super-mathematician Tarnec Brodix destroys his universe, and the fault spreads into the Earth universe in the form of a Dark Tide of Absolute Nothingness. Unable to save himself, Brodix transfers his knowledge into the one mind powerful enough to receive it: that if Sefian, the son who has been born to Viona and Quorne. Sefian rapidly evolves, and, no longer human, after saving the Earth universe, vanishes into the greater universe, to seek new challenges. Then the Amazon is confronted with a further puzzle—a large section of the planet Neptune is discovered to be an exact duplicate of the Earth!

Book Six: *Quorne Returns*

The bacterial intelligences of Neptune plan to conquer Earth by replacing humans in key positions with alien duplicates. The Neptunians are themselves subjugated by the sinister Atlantean scientist, Sefner Quorne. Alerted to the threat, the Golden Amazon hits back by creating the ultimate doomsday weapon—only to precipitate a reprisal from the denizens of another universe....

Book Seven: *The Central Intelligence*

The Golden Amazon's arch-enemy, Sefner Quorne, discovers that all mental gifts, such as memory and creativity, are something that is broadcast throughout the universe by a Central Intelligence—and then interpreted according to the quality of the individual brain of the recipient. At the surprising suggestion of his wife, Viona, the Amazon's daughter, Quorne travels with her to the very center of the universe, in order to wrest the secrets of mentality from the very source itself!

Book Eight: *The Cosmic Crusaders*

The Golden Amazon renounces all ties with Earth when, together with her husband, Abna, and her daughter, Viona, she sets off on a journey to explore the cosmos. On the strange worlds of Alpha Centauri, she encounters Mizanu, the embodiment of evil—a planet-sized hypertrophied brain! Its baleful, crushing mental power threatens to reach out beyond the double-system of Alpha and Proxima Centauri to engulf the Earth and all the other inhabited planets of the galaxy—unless the Amazon can destroy it first!

Book Nine: *Parasite Planet*

The Cosmic Crusaders discover a fantastic world of mental parasites drawing form and substance from our own Earth, fifty light years distant. The planet is ruled by a being identical to the Golden Amazon herself—but an Amazon who's coldly scientific and vicious, mirroring the original Amazon as she had once been early in her career. Inevitably, they become locked in a deadly duel—to the death!

Book Ten: *World Out of Step*

The Cosmic Crusaders find themselves on a planet that seems mysteriously not to conform with natural law, a world out of step with the universe. It leaps ahead into time at unexpected moments, thereby suddenly adding many years of age to the flower-like inhabitants, and killing tens of thousands of individuals through death and old age. In trying to find the alien menace responsible, The Golden Amazon and her fellow Crusaders are flung backwards and forwards through time and space, threatening their own survival....

Book Eleven: *The Shadow People*

The Cosmic Crusaders discover a planet whose people are subject to a baleful influence from outer space that sweeps across their world—and for a brief while embraces every man, woman and child. It stirs the emotions of the sexes against each other. Men desire only to destroy women, and women men. Only those with higher types of mind are able to build a resistance against it. The struggle is dire and dreadful, and leaves its victims physical and mental wrecks. The less fortunate are left dead after the Wave has passed.

But when the Crusaders identify and destroy the source of the problem, they precipitate an even greater menace....

CHAPTER ONE
THE SILVER PLANET

Abna, the majestic, seven-foot giant of faraway Jupiter, sat brooding. Around him were all the resources of the *Ultra*'s control room; before him a mass of calculations. There was not a sound, since the *Ultra* was cruising in the free void, far away in the spawning depths of the Milky Way.

"Strange," Abna mused, turning back to his figures. "It doesn't seem a normal thing."

"What doesn't?"

He glanced up and smiled. The Golden Amazon had just entered the control room, that never-aging woman of superhuman strength and phenomenal beauty who was Abna's wife.

"I've just been making calculations on this silver planet," Abna explained. "See what you think of my maths."

"Wouldn't be much use," the Amazon shrugged. "When it comes to mathematics I have to admit you are my superior.... What conclusion have you come to?"

"One very clear one. That the curious magnetism it

seems to emit is an illusory one. Viewing the planet, we feel drawn towards it. There is a conviction of happiness about it—as though everything that happened on that world is of the sheerest joy. But it's wrong, you know. Utterly wrong."

"How—wrong?"

"It is emanating a series of radiations, most of which I can't classify, and one of them has the effect of gearing up our nerves to intense exhilaration. Same as drink and drugs do back on Earth in some measure. It isn't genuine: it's a physical reaction."

The Amazon nodded thoughtfully, and then turned to the enormous observation window. Standing there, with the stars visible through the flawless glass behind her, she seemed to Abna like a goddess for a moment. Which, in a sense, she was. The most extraordinary woman ever born on Earth, she was now the leader of the Cosmic Crusaders, a quartet committed to the self-imposed task of bringing scientific knowledge and uplift to distant worlds, a quartet comprised of herself, her husband, her daughter Viona, and Mexone—Viona's husband. And it was the fact of being a Cosmic Crusader that caused the Amazon to now reflect deeply.

"Are we justified," she asked presently, "in using our time and energies to explore a world that emits illusory waves? Would we be wasting our time?"

"Depends if the planet's inhabited," Abna answered. "Still more, it depends what sort of civilization—if any—is in existence there."

"You haven't seen any signs of civilization?"

"Not yet. We're still too far away." Abna rose and crossed over to the window. He put an arm about the Amazon's shoulders and gazed with her into the incomprehensible deeps of space.

"We haven't been traveling long toward that planet," Abna added. "No more than two hours."

The Amazon nodded silently. Her eyes were fixed on the world in question—a dazzlingly bright solitary point, with no trace of a sun near it. Its brilliance was such that Venus, when seen from Earth, would have been but a candle flame by comparison.

"Strange what a tremendous albedo it has," the Amazon mused, lapsing into the technical term for light-reflection. "Considering that there is no sun near it."

Abna nodded absently, then he gave a start. Something was coming in sight in the void ahead, a little to the left of the solitary mystery planet. In a matter of seconds the 'something' had transformed itself into a stupendous brilliance, growing ever brighter. Before long it had paled even the bright planet.

"What is it?" the Amazon asked in surprise, narrowing her eyes.

Abna gave no immediate answer. Instead he hurried to the nearby wall rack, took down a couple of pairs of blue goggles, and handed one pair to the Amazon. Their eyes thus protected, the two studied the phenomenon.

"Now I get it," Abna said finally. "There is a sun lighting that planet—and that blinding spot of light is it. Up to now it was eclipsed from our view because of some dark world in between. Now it's moved aside, we can see the sun clearly."

Such indeed seemed to be the case. The sun of the mystery bright world was only a small one—but of tremendously intense power. Abna studied it in puzzlement for a while, then crossed to the instrument panel. In a moment he switched on an automatic analyzer. The Amazon, pushing her goggles up on to her forehead, came across and joined him, watching the faintly humming machinery intently.

"Now let's see...." Abna looked at a display on the instrument, frowning over the readings.

"High magnesium content," the Amazon commented. "That accounts for the brilliance."

"Accounts for the sun, yes—but not for the planet. Magnesium only reveals its brilliance when in the gaseous flame state. Normally it is gray and has hardly any albedo. Must be something else to account for the planet's brightness."

Returning her goggles to her eyes, the Amazon went back to the window.

"Obviously," she said at length, "that sun is nearer to us than the planet—in fact, it has to be, otherwise the planet would be half- or quarter-lighted. And it isn't. The whole disc is illuminated."

"And apparently there are no other planets in the system," Abna added. "That in itself is queer. A one-planet system—or two-, if we count that hulk which was causing the eclipse—is something we haven't come across yet. Wonder where the others are?"

The Amazon shrugged. "Since we can't answer that, let's concentrate on what we've got. Any chance of telescopic examination?"

"Certainly; but I think we'd better wait until we're a bit nearer. We're 120 million miles away. I'll put on speed and bring our wondering to an end."

When presently they had crossed the orbit of the dead planet, which had formerly been eclipsing the sun, the Amazon turned.

"That definitely makes it a two-planet system, Abna. That planet, though, is just a burned-out hulk of rock without any air or water. Wonder what happened to devastate it to that extent?"

Abna did not answer. He was too busy focusing the powerful telescope. At length he got it to his liking, and a blurry image came into view on the scanning screen. A twist of a knob and the view was sharply defined.

"Come and look," he said briefly, and the Amazon moved to his side.

Silent, they stood surveying the mystery world, the glare of the sun rending the left-hand side misty and indistinct. But they could see enough, such as is was. There seemed to be thousands of tiny squares in the midst of an intolerably bright sea, squares that made neither sense nor reason.

"Any suggestions?" the Amazon asked presently, her eyes beginning to ache with the glare.

"Not yet. Those blobs in an apparently molten sea

don't make any sense—unless they're mountains or something. Try later when we're still nearer."

"If the planet's molten, it's no use carrying on," the Amazon said. "Anyway, we'll see what happens."

This they did, in another two hours when they had come measurably nearer the planet. A second telescopic observation was made, and this time it was perfectly clear that the planet was not molten, but covered with some brilliantly gleaming substance. By this time the various squares and queer formations had resolved themselves into buildings—of sorts. Queer sort of buildings, mainly square and very crude. If there were any inhabitants, the distance was still too great for the telescope to pick them up.

"Atmosphere's all right," the Amazon said, busy with the analyzer. "About the same as Earth. So also is the gravity. The only thing against our landing on that world is the glare. Think we'll be able to stand it? Even at this distance we need these blue goggles."

Abna did not answer the question directly. Instead he said: "The more I study this world the more sure I become that it's made of some precious metal—eroded and polished to enormous brilliance by the action of wind and weather. And the metal, I think, is silver."

The Amazon reflected. "Well, it's possible, I suppose. We can find out when we land—if our eyes will stand it. How long before we touch down?"

"About three hours. We'd better tell Viona and Mexone, then they can be ready."

The Amazon duly alerted the two, who were deeply

sleeping. Presently they came into the control room and without pause, crossed to the observation window, to immediately recoil from it at the terrific glare that smote their eyes.

Viona gasped. "That planet's just like a huge mirror reflecting the sunlight."

"Pretty nearly," Abna agreed, handing over two pairs of goggles. "With a combination of a magnesium-rich sun and a silver world, you're bound to get plenty of brilliance."

"Silver?" Mexone repeated in surprise.

"To the best of my belief, yes. I think that planet—the surface anyway—is entirely composed of it—and polished, too, with wind action."

Viona and Mexone turned back to an examination of the world toward which the *Ultra* was swiftly speeding. Presently the Amazon also came into the control room, a weapon belt now buckled around her slender waist.

"I don't know if there's life, but there's nothing like being prepared," she explained, then she crossed to the telescope, focused it swiftly, and stood looking at the reflector-screen.

This time the crude buildings were much clearer, and now the distance had diminished, there were also signs of specks. Sometimes they were in considerable numbers, sometimes isolated. What was immediately apparent was their movement.

"Life!" the Amazon announced. "Beings of some sort. From the way they congregate and the sort of buildings they have, I'd say nomadic tribes."

Pushing up their goggles, Viona and Mexone swiftly joined her. In silent interest they both took in the view reflected in the screen.

"Whether it's worth visiting or not I still don't know," the Amazon said finally, at which Viona looked up sharply.

"No question of it, surely? Even if we don't advance these people materially, we're adding to our store of knowledge, and that's something. Besides, it'll save us dying of boredom."

"I don't think we'll ever do that," Abna commented dryly.

"Conditions, except for the light, are favorable for exploration," the Amazon said, and outlined what she and Abna had already discovered about the planet.

"And the only other planet in the system is burned out?" Viona asked, puzzled.

"Entirely. Even more of a hulk than our moon is."

"Wonder why? May be a simple explanation—or a grim one." Suddenly she swung eagerly to Abna. "Hurry up, dad, and let's land! I'm sure there'll be something interesting."

"You mean you think there will," Abna corrected. "At the moment you're experiencing an unusually high elation—but it's only superficial. Doesn't mean a thing."

"Oh?" Viona's sapphire blue eyes clouded for a moment. "Well, if it's only phony, it's certainly got a kick. I feel on top of the world—which sounds rather idiotic way out in the Milky Way," she concluded, smiling.

"Better arm yourselves," the Amazon instructed. "There may be trouble. In any case, there's no sense in being unprepared."

Viona and Mexone both nodded, and for the next few moments were busy strapping instrument and weapon belts about their waists. Then Viona looked in surprise as the Amazon held out two pairs of goggles.

"From the look of things you're going to need them," she explained. "In fact, we all are. The glare reflected from snow is mere twilight compared to this lot."

Silently the two younger ones slipped the goggles on to their foreheads; then spent the rest of the time just waiting. Abna remained at the control board while the Amazon, her goggles in place, stared down on that incredibly bright world and tried at the same time to fathom her emotions. Had she been a normal woman, she would have realized that she had risen to the point of almost hysterical ecstasy—an abandoned sense in which nothing mattered. Being possessed of a coldly scientific streak, however, she analyzed the condition for what it was and refused to let herself be misled by its promptings. Just the same, she was puzzled.

So presently the *Ultra*, its velocity lowered to normal flying speed, came into the atmosphere of the planet and thereafter swiftly cleaved downwards toward the brilliant landscape. The Amazon, Viona, and Mexone watched intently, goggles in position, as an agglomeration of the crudely fashioned dwellings came into view.

"Queer sort of planet," the Amazon commented

thoughtfully. "It has a revolution of roughly twenty-two hours: I've checked on that, so we'll get some relief from the glare when the night comes. But as to the landscape, words fail me. Now we're so near it seems certain that everything except the dwellings is silver."

"Be worth a bit back home," Viona mused.

"I wonder," the Amazon reflected. "Dump this much silver on the markets of the world and the stuff would not be worth a cent. Remember, it is rarity that makes for value."

With a mighty rushing of air against the invincible outer walls, the machine hurtled downwards and over the first mass of buildings and came to rest. Once it touched ground, it noticeably slithered like a car on a wet roadway. Then with a jerk it halted.

Silence. The power plant was cut off and from outside there were no sounds. The four crowded around the observation window, gazing at the distant remnants of the crude buildings. They were little better than cottages, or even mid-African villages. Certainly they did not suggest a high form of civilization. Behind them, glittering mountains rose up like creations of a wonderland, with a cobalt blue cloudless sky beyond.

"Pretty—but confoundedly bright," Viona muttered. Then she lifted her goggles and looked with her normal eyes. The glare was hurtful but not so penetrating as she had expected.

Seeing her action, the Amazon, Abna, and Mexone followed suit, then glanced at each other in surprise.

"No worse than white pavements at high noon," the

Amazon said at length "Wonder why? In space we couldn't stand to even look at it."

The Amazon seemed about to make further comment, then she stopped herself as the first evidences of life on this queer world became evident. In the far distance, coming from the direction of the dwellings, was a running horde of people, advancing with all the excitement and energy of savages on the warpath. Yet, in a sense, they did not appear savage: quite the contrary. There was a certain childlike enthusiasm about their activity as they swept nearer and nearer.

In a very few minutes they had reached the *Ultra* and begun to assemble around it. More came from the distance, until at last there must have been several hundred. In silence the quartet looked out on them from the higher elevation of the observation window.

"For some reason," the Amazon said, "I'm reminded of one Gulliver on the island of Lilliput.'"

There was a certain amount of logic in her simile. The people were all small-statured, yet exactly like Earth people in their formation. Their attire was extremely scanty, but in certain cases was embellished with crude armlets and anklets of the all-prevailing silver metal. In actual appearance they were somehow immature— with smooth, laughing faces and hair crudely cut. At the moment they seemed to be having a good deal of amusement prancing around the machine and grinning and gesticulating to one another.

"They are not mature people," the Amazon said at length, with a trace of disappointment. "They're behaving exactly like ten-year-old children. I had somehow hoped for clever scientists. I suppose we must stay here?"

"All the more reason why we should, I think," Viona commented. "Their development is such as to show that they are adult, both the men and the women—but their intelligence doesn't match it. Seems to me it's up to us to find out why."

"Childlike adults on a world of silver," Abna sighed. "What next, I wonder?" He moved to the airlock switch. "All right, here we go!"

The ponderous airlock swung open very slowly, and the four made to stride forward—but that was as far as they got. Like children suddenly told of a candy horde, the little people came surging into the ship, laughing and chattering amongst themselves, until the control room was full of them. It left the quartet towering up like islands amidst a flood, and for a moment they stood watching curiously, weighing up these beings of a fantastic planet.

Children with adult bodies! There was no getting away from it. They were mature all right, yet their actions and emotions were miles behind their physical development.

They seemed quite suddenly to become aware of the visitors and when they did so they fell back quickly, as though realizing they had in some way perhaps committed an indiscretion. Big-eyed and wondering, they stood waiting—crowding out through the airlock into the brilliantly sunny spaces outside.

"Friends," Abna said deliberately, pointing to himself and then the others. "We come as friends. Can you understand me?"

Apparently not, from the blank looks that greeted him. And, typically childlike, one or two of the little people giggled to themselves, either at the heavy timbre of Abna's voice, or else his enormous height.

"Kids!" the Amazon sighed regretfully. "I think we ought to be on our way, Abna. We're not school teachers."

"We haven't finished yet," Abna responded. "Just because our experiences up to now have brought us into contact with highly developed civilizations, it's no reason for ignoring one that's exactly the opposite.... Anyway, the language difficulty is no problem. Viona, switch on the Educator."

Viona reached out a slim hand and obliged. The eyes of the little people immediately turned to one of the countless machines ranged against the wall—and in particular to one that resembled a gigantic helmet with a chair fixed beneath it.

"Exchange information?" the Amazon questioned. "Force our language upon them?"

"Exactly." Abna nodded briefly; then suddenly he lunged out and caught one of the little men by the arm. It was simple to force him, obviously not a little frightened, to the chair beneath the instrument. Clamps dropped in place and prevented him from escaping.

"No harm intended," Abna smiled at him, and though he knew his words were unintelligible, they seemed nevertheless to have an effect, for the little man relaxed and waited.

"Right," Abna nodded, and again Viona reached to the control panel and applied the power. There was no sound save a faint humming, but all the time it persisted the quartet knew that every detail of their own basic language was being engraved indelibly on the little man's brain—a fact quite obvious from the astounded expression on his face. He was no longer frightened, but bewildered.

Abna signaled, and the hum of power ceased. The little man sat limply in his chair, not unconscious but with all the fight and energy knocked out of him.

"You are not hurt, my friend?" Abna asked quietly; and the big blue eyes turned to him.

"No—not hurt." The words were used awkwardly, and plainly for the first time. "I am wondering what miracle it is that enables you to do this to me—to transfer your language into my brain without the need of learning."

"That is but one of the many miracles of which we are capable, my friend. As you will have gathered, we are from another world, and we come peacefully to exchange information with you."

The little man nodded slowly and then looked at his gaping colleagues. Men and women alike were watching in dazed silence.

"From what world do you come?" the little man asked.

"Far away, my friend—many light-years. It is not

important. Your world attracted us, so we came to it. We would like to know more about it."

"There is not much to tell. This planet is called Tuca, and we are the descendants of the Asronians, a race of great scientists who unfortunately were a trifle too brilliant for their own good."

Abna frowned with sudden interest. Holding out his hand, he helped the little man from his chair to a standing position, and seemingly conscious that he alone had been singled out for the great moment, the little man stood erect and proud.

"My name is Doxa," he said, and inclined his head of thick woolly black hair in a slight obeisance.

"Abna, the Golden Amazon, Viona, and Mexone," Abna said, indicating his own quartet. "Now we understand each other better. It would seem there is a good deal more you can tell me, Doxa—if you will."

"It will be a pleasure, wondrous stranger—but first I would make a request. Might others of my fellows, men and women, undergo the marvelous language experience that they, too, might converse? My own particular friends?"

Abna smiled an acknowledgement, thereupon Doxa reverted to his own language and singled out half a dozen men and women from the assembly. Each in turn underwent the rigors of the Educator and emerged wide-eyed and knowledgeable.

"That's all?" Abna asked, looking at the three men and three women; then at Doxa.

"That is enough," Doxa said ambiguously. "Were I

to include any more they would know as much as I do, and that would not be sensible. My friends and I, having now the power to converse with you, have also the control of our fellows."

Abna nodded slowly. "Because you have the knowledge? I understand."

"We have needed something like this," Doxa said slowly. "Something that would give to one of us—or a picked body of us—a little extra knowledge, thereby making it right that we should be rulers. Up to now nobody has ruled, and the outcome has been something approaching chaos."

"Which you can remedy?" the Amazon inquired.

"Exactly. But come with me, friends, and consider yourselves entirely welcome. Your machine will be perfectly safe."

Although Abna was reasonably sure of the fact, he did not neglect to leave the controls completely locked: then he watched as the crowd of little men and women filed out through the airlock.

"Any idea what we're getting into?" the Amazon asked.

"Not the slightest—but if we can't deal with an army of pygmies if they get tough, we must be slipping. Let's go."

With that Abna followed the crowd through the glare of the magnesium sunlight. He took one fleeting glimpse of it sailing, at the zenith in the cobalt sky. Then he began to follow the chattering, laughing crowd across the metallic plain in the direction of the crudely built buildings. Almost in the center of them stood a massive, tall needle of silver with a ledge near its top. Perhaps it was an observation post, some kind of totem pole, or even a pagan god. It was difficult to say.

"I think you're right about this stuff being silver," Viona said, coming up. "It's incredible, but true."

"Might take that pillar away with us against a rainy day," Abna chuckled; then he caught the Amazon's cold, disapproving glance.

"For a man many times a multimillionaire that's a crazy remark," she commented. "That exhilaration radiation must be working overtime on you."

"It is," Abna admitted. "I see no particular reason to resist it, either. I feel most remarkably cheerful, and it's obvious that these child-people feel likewise. If this planet were not so far from Earth it would make an excellent health resort."

The Amazon closed the distance between herself and Abna and then she lowered her voice a little.

"Did you make anything of Doxa's remark that these people—and himself—are descendants of the Asronians?"

"I made nothing of it at all. Maybe we will later."

And Abna did not attempt to concentrate any further. Nor for that matter did the Amazon. The curious exhilaration that the planet produced made anything concentrative too much effort. It was so much easier to succumb and let things be.

Finally, somewhat dazzled by the brilliance of the metal plain, the party reached the outermost of the odd-looking buildings, and here Doxa called a halt. He shouted a few words to the crowd, with the result that they all dispersed quickly to different buildings— then, with his six colleagues on either side of him, he faced the travelers.

"I would suggest that we dine and confer at the same time," he said. "This is my home, to which you are fully welcome."

His choice of words in the language that had been 'wished' on him was somewhat peculiar but the meaning was clear. And his pomp and ceremony was also almost amusing. Abna and the Amazon nodded gravely and stepped into the low-roofed dwelling, with Viona and Mexone close behind them.

Within, the habitation was surprisingly roomy, though the roof was low. There was a small amount of fairly earthly looking furniture, and the walls were crudely decorated. The surprising thing was that the edifice was built of timber—very roughly and amateur- ishly built, too—and not of the all-prevailing silver. Two windows gave adequate illumination, considering the tremendous power of the external sunlight.

"Be seated," Doxa invited, with a flourish—and after some maneuvering of the odd chairs, the quartet managed to fix themselves up. Doxa waited until they were seated, then he gave a sign that promptly caused his six followers to sit cross-legged on the wooden floor. The resemblance to children playing some kind of game at a party could not be avoided.

"Now you shall have food, my friends," Doxa

decided, and going to the door of his dwelling he gave an all-powerful cry in his own language. This done, he returned and sat cross-legged at the head of his retinue.

"I appoint myself as leader, therefore I shall do the talking," he said, with a cherubic smile. "We, the Asronians, have never had a leader before. Leadership comes by knowing something more than the next man, by being singled out for a certain purpose. I have been thus singled out; therefore, I shall be leader."

At the close of this speech he looked around on his followers as though expecting dissent, but none came. Satisfied, he folded his arms and endeavored to look dignified. The effect was somewhat seriocomic.

"Speak, travelers from a distant world. What do you wish to know?"

"You speak of yourselves as 'descendants'," Abna said slowly. "What happened to your predecessors?"

"Originally," Doxa said, "there was the most powerful race of scientists in the Universe on this planet. If that sounds ego—ego—" He hesitated over the word, then took a deep breath. "If that sounds egotistical, it is not meant to. They were geniuses, every man and woman of them. But too clever for their own good."

Doxa paused and froze into silence as two women appeared with food on trays. Strangely enough, it was meat, though there had as yet been no sign of animals around. There were implements to eat it with, and a kind of wine. The trays were set down on the floor and the women departed.

"I trust our food is correct for your type of physique,"

Doxa remarked anxiously, and waited while Abna tested it.

"Yes—excellent," Abna smiled. "Our thanks to you, Doxa, though we are wondering where the meat came from."

"A small animal much prevalent in the underground," Doxa explained. "Our main staple meat diet. The animals multiply very rapidly, except when the giant beasts arouse themselves and enjoy an orgy of destruction."

Since the four had not the least idea what Doxa was talking about, they let the matter drop and tackled the food. And very palatable it proved to be.

"You were saying," the Amazon remarked, "that your ancestors were geniuses."

"Ah, yes. Not so very long ago, either—certainly within the memory of the oldest of us here—the race flourished. This world and the neighbor world of Antara were thickly populated, and housed many wonderful scientific machines."

"And then?" Abna prompted, as there was a long silence.

"Then something happened. On both Antara and here there was a devastating explosion, followed by devouring fire, which generated overwhelming heat. Antara was totally destroyed and is now nothing but a burned-out hulk. On this world the great cities and machines of metal were melted level with the ground, which accounts for our metallic crust. Out of the holocaust only a few survived. They were numb with shock, and no longer possessed of tremendous genius. A few of them babbled of an experiment to change the probability of electronic waves, but that fact did not mean anything to anybody...." Doxa shrugged.

"The survivors soon died off, leaving behind the children who grew to maturity. Us!" he concluded, and gave his broad, infantile smile.

"Change the probability of electronic waves," the Amazon repeated thoughtfully. "And did they succeed in doing this?"

"I believe not. Something went wrong, which accounted for the terrifying fire and wholesale destruction...." Doxa became thoughtful for a moment and seemed to be making an effort to think and speak maturely. "It was, so to speak, an experiment by a race which had achieved absolute perfection. Absolute perfection had caused boredom, the lack of anything fresh to conquer. Being dissatisfied with this state of affairs, the idea of changing electronic probability was conceived—with diabolic results. The race just vanished."

"And you made no endeavor to emulate the mighty feats of your ancestors?" Abna inquired. "You prefer to live as children, without a single responsibility?"

Doxa giggled. "We do, yes. We have constructed our dwellings, which, though crude, are serviceable in a climate that never alters. We have food and drink enough, so why should we saddle ourselves with responsibility and knowledge? Then there is always the feeling of elation, the feeling of perfect health, the absolute sureness that all is well."

Obviously, Doxa had not tumbled to the fact that there was a curious radiation about the planet that caused this high-springing of the emotions. Even more obviously, he had never attempted to keep the feeling under control.

"And finally," Doxa finished, "there is always the transport of the gods. If they smile upon us, there comes a time when we are lifted away to Paradise, never even tasting the anguish of death."

His giggling ceased as he spoke and a curious expression came to his face. At the same moment the quartet looked up sharply, all of them sensing a mysterious tension in the atmosphere. They could not quite pinpoint what it was—even less where it came from, but one thing they did know.

Doxa was becoming transparent! Even as he sat there his solid little form misted, became ghostly, and then he was gone. His colleagues looked for a moment at the spot where he had been—their faces frozen into complete immobility, then with one accord they all scrambled from their squatting positions and bowed in deep obeisance to the blank spot where Doxa had been seated.

CHAPTER TWO
INTO THE UNDERWORLD

It took several moments for the quartet to recover from their astonishment. A multitude of questions occurred to them, but they refrained from asking them because the disappearing act seemed to be something quite normal to the little people. Even now they were settling themselves on the floor.

"What happened?" Abna asked at length.

One of the little men, who had taken up the position formerly occupied by Doxa, looked up seriously. He was plainly a man of less intelligence than Doxa, and indeed not so good-humored. Up to now he had rarely smiled, his general expression being one of vaguely puzzled solemnity.

"I rule in Doxa's place," he said, and apparently he assumed there was no doubt about it. "My name is Scind. I believe that our brother Doxa spoke too much and too freely, but now he has gone to Paradise, there is nothing more to be said. You will not find me quite so communicative, my friends."

Abna completely brushed aside the man's obvious unpleasantness with another question.

"Did you say Paradise?"

"I did." The little man's cold green eyes were vaguely belligerent. "Did he not tell you himself that occasionally one or other of us is lifted to Paradise without tasting death? The gods smiled on him, and it happened. Odd it should come so quickly on his statements."

"Very odd," the Amazon said grimly. "And if you expect us to believe he's gone to Paradise, you're much mistaken."

"Steady, Vi," Abna murmured. "No use stirring up trouble. I think we'll find it fast enough as it is." He cleared his throat and addressed Scind again. "The exact reason for Doxa's disappearance we don't pretend to understand, but we are prepared to let it be.… Let us get down to other matters. You say you've taken control in Doxa's place?"

"I have!"

"Then because this is an alien planet, we must ask your permission before doing anything. Briefly, we would like to stay for a while and explore. You will not be incommoded. We will use our spaceship as our base."

Scind reflected for a moment or two, then finally he gave a rather surly nod.

"If you wish. You will find there is little to explore."

To this Abna did not respond. Getting to his feet, he jerked his head to the others and led the way out of the dwelling. When at length they had wandered some distance amid the crude habitations, watched curiously but inoffensively by the little people, Abna slowed his pace somewhat.

"I think," he said, as the Amazon, Viona, and Mexone fell into step with him, "that we're going to find something interesting here. That 'trip to Paradise' illusion was the neatest thing I've seen for some time."

"For myself," the Amazon said, "I'm inclined to doubt that the thing was an illusion. Seemed perfectly natural to me, even though as yet I don't know the why or wherefore."

Abna pondered as he walked along, considering the smooth, brilliantly glittering silver under his feet.

"That sense of exaltation is still with us," he commented. "We know it must be a radiation of some kind, and I'm pretty sure it isn't from the sun. So it must come from a machine somewhere. That make sense?"

"Yes," replied Viona. "Except that we haven't seen a machine in all our explorations."

"Our explorations have been conducted from the air. We haven't seen animals either, yet Doxa assured us that there are some, both small and large. Since they are apparently below the surface, it is possible that a machine would be below surface, too. In fact, highly probable, considering that all the cities were reduced to a molten mass of silver which later hardened into what we now behold."

"Even if there were such a machine, what good would it do us to find it?"

"I don't know, but I was thinking that if we could

discover the reason for this emotion of ecstasy, we might duplicate it and use it on Earth. Such a contrivance would save many people from acute depression and melancholia. Don't forget, that apart from crusading, we're willing to pick up any inventions that are of use to us. This may be such a case."

The Amazon thought it out as they came beyond the confines of the 'settlement,' and had brilliantly lighted, glittering plain before them.

"Yes, there's something in it," she admitted at length. "And do you realize the enormity of the experiment these scientists were engaged upon? Nothing less than changing the probability waves of the electron! Why, if they had succeeded, they might have altered the entire pattern of the Universe! One cannot change one electron without there being universal repercussions. Every electron is essential in its own way.'"

"Exactly," Abna said, with a quiet grimness—and there was something in his expression that brought the Amazon to a stop.

"Out with it, Abna!" she said bluntly. "You've something on your mind. What is it?"

"It's this. I'm wondering if the scientists were overwhelmed before their experiment was complete. As far as we can gather, there was uncontrollable fire and a devastating explosion, which wiped out the neighbor planet and melted the cities on this planet. That may have been the early stages of the effort to alter electron paths. After that the scientists ceased to have any interest in the proceedings by reason of being dead. All their works were buried under a flood of molten silver, on the surface of which their successors proceeded to live as childlike adults.... Make sense so far?"

"Entirely," the Amazon confirmed. "Go on."

"There is an underground to this world, in which animals, large and small, have their existence," Abna continued. "Doxa told us that much. That may probably be the region where the scientists originally worked before the collapse of their cities overwhelmed them. Second, we have an undoubted radiation from somewhere which produces elation, and we have also mysterious disappearances, as witness Doxa."

"You think the disappearance might have been caused by electronic probability changes?" Viona asked quickly.

"Scientifically, since it was certainly not an illusion, it could not have been caused by anything else! I am led to think that the electron-shifting machinery is still at work, and that it is responsible for the disappearances—for it seems there have been others—and the elation effect as well."

"I apologize," Mexone said. "You forget that even yet I am not thoroughly acquainted with your aims and science. What exactly is meant by changing electronic probability?"

"Probability," Abna said, "is in truth the foundation of the material universe and everything within it. No scientist has ever seen an electron, and it is unlikely if any scientist ever will. Even granting a microscope powerful enough to see an electron, the very act of using light to view it would deflect it from its position. So from that there arises the Law of Probability—namely, that an electron is only inferred and not seen."

"I understand that," Mexone said. "What else?"

"Everything inorganic and organic is made up of electrons," Abna resumed. "It is inferred that a certain number of electrons in a certain place will make up a certain object—and most times it is so. But have a machine of unusual qualities, probably employing disturbing electrical waves, and electrons may not fall into the pattern required. In other words, the probability that they will form—or have formed—such and such a pattern will yield to a different probability entirely and the expected object either dematerializes, as in the case of Doxa, or doesn't materialize at all. Once given that uncertainly, it can be and is progressive. One disturbed center of electrons affects another and so sets up a chain reaction, which disturbs every electron in the universe. And rapidly, too, since the interchange is made at the speed of light, or 186,000 miles a second."

"How do you foresee any danger from such a machine?" Mexone asked, shrugging. "You seem to have a pretty complete idea of what it is doing. With no scientists present to interfere, it will remain as it is now, won't it?"

Abna shook his head slowly. "No. It will reach a state when all the possible probabilities have been exhausted, and when that happens some new conception will take place. I don't know what, but it might be far-reaching. Anything dealing with electronics in this form always is. We would be well advised to try to get at the machine and study it."

Abna in the lead, they began moving over the hard, glittering plain. Presently the glare became so intolerable that they slipped on their dark goggles and thereafter viewed the brilliant landscape through a restful violet glow. Since it was getting into late afternoon, the sun was naturally lower and its light was positively blinding when reflected from the vast areas of smoothly polished silver.

Without speaking, the quartet moved farther and farther away from the 'settlement,' but they were always linked to the *Ultra* by their compass instruments, which unfailingly pointed to the spaceship wherever they might be.

"Correct me if I'm wrong," Mexone said at length, "but are we coming to a kind of valley ahead?"

"We are," the Amazon confirmed. "I've been looking at it for some time."

The possibility of a change in the monotony of the landscape set them hurrying forward more urgently, and within twenty minutes they had come to the 'valley.' It was not a true valley but a gigantic crack in the silver, the same kind of crack which one would find in the contraction of lava during the cooling process. It went down into darkness since, by now, the sun failed to reach in to the depths.

"It may be a false cleft, or it may lead down into the real underworld," the Amazon said at length, and then she contemplated the sheer, smooth, metal walls.

"And it seems to run the length of the planet," Abna mused, looking right and left. "At least as far as we can see. It means we either go down or turn back. What's it to be?"

"Ever hear of the Crusaders turning back?" Viona asked in amazement. "We go down—naturally. Our goggles are dual use, with a built-in headlamp. We've got ropes, and we're not exactly amateurs at mountaineering."

"But this isn't like descending an ordinary crevice," the Amazon pointed out. "There's no toe and finger hold whatever. Just a sheer face of silver."

Viona shrugged as she pulled a coil of nylon rope from her belt.

"Must touch bottom somewhere," she said. "Let's go."

"I'll go first," Abna decided, pushing his goggles on to his forehead and switching on the tiny but immensely powerful inset torch. "The rest of you watch that my rope is safe."

He looked back at where it was lodged in a smaller crevice by means of a hook anchor; then he gently pulled on it to be sure it was a tight fixture. Satisfied, he began to lower himself over the silver lip and thereafter went down with his legs scissored around the thin but amazingly tough rope…. Down he went, his headlamp blazing in the darkness—down, and still down.

"Seems a long way," Viona commented, watching intently.

Mexone and the Amazon did not say anything, even though they were in agreement with her. Abna still went down, and the light of his atomic lamp was no more than a mere pinprick when at last there came the jerk on the rope that announced he had touched bottom.

Immediately the Amazon began to follow him—and Viona and Mexone followed quickly afterwards—until finally the four of them were standing on solid silver again, looking at each other in the torchlight.

"Well, what now?" the Amazon asked, her manner indicating that she was still out of sympathy with the whole exploration. "We don't seem to have gained much. From the look of things we're simply in the bottom of a cleft which leads nowhere."

"So it seems," Abna sighed. "Well, we didn't know until we looked."

Viona, however, was still unsatisfied. She had the natural curiosity of youth and for that reason began moving slowly to the right, her head-torch providing a brilliant beam of light into an excessively narrow cleft that marked the base of the chasm. Mexone came slowly behind her, and on each side the walls loomed in flashing silver, an unbelievable El Dorado.

"What's the idea?" Mexone asked.

"I'm interested in that," Viona explained, and pointed to a narrow, roughly oval black mark some way ahead, sunken into the wall.

Mexone looked, and then nodded. In a moment or two they had reached the mark—and even as Viona had anticipated it was an actual hole in the silver, very crudely made. Quickly she put her head and shoulders through the gap and gazed into a black wilderness beyond, except within the immediate area of the lamplight.

It was a strange sight that Viona beheld. Around her were towering pinnacles of normal rock, spliced with veins of silver. The 100 percent silver formation was not present down here, but instead there were the natural materials of the planet. Everything seemed to be a wilderness of stalactites, monstrous silver-veined spears suspended from the roof of an enormous natural cavern.

"Mmmm, very interesting," Viona told herself, and her voice boomed hollowly; then she endeavored to wriggle herself further through the hole. Being slim, she had not much difficulty, but when she got as far as her hips, enlarged by the instrument belt, she was jammed. Her hands flailed uselessly amidst rock and silver chippings as she made a frantic effort to drag herself through. She did not particularly notice what she was clutching in her agitated struggles, but presently she desisted in her efforts as a low grumbling sound reached her.

Startled, she jerked up her head. At the same moment there was a distinct quaking motion. She stared, bewildered, then it struck her that her hands had clawed away various rock supports—natural ones—upon which higher rocks had been resting. As a result, the whole wall was on the move. She had, in effect, begun an avalanche.

It took her ten seconds to realize this fact, and probably another three to apprehend that immediately above her was a gigantic needle of silver and rock slowly slipping downwards, its merciless point directly overhead. Once it slipped the whole distance from the rocks at present imprisoning it—!

"Viona! What's wrong?" bawled Mexone's voice from beyond the hole. "Get through, can't you?"

The danger snapped Viona back into action. With all the strength at her command she tugged and strained to get forward and free herself, without success. And to move back was equally impossible.

"Help me, somebody!" screamed Viona's muffled voice. "There's a rock coming down on top of me! Get me out!"

As the ground heaved gently to the accompaniment of a deep growling rumble the Amazon leaped forward and seized Viona's legs tightly. Then she pulled—and pulled again, but it was no use. Viona's waist was securely wedged into the silver hole.

"Quick, Abna!" the Amazon's face was tense. "There's plenty of trouble coming from the sound of things and we've got to get Viona clear. Cut the hole round her body."

"Right! But it won't be easy."

He pulled out his proton gun, narrowed the nozzle to the smallest point, and then pressed the button. A needle-thin line of fire projected at the hole around Viona's waist and began to cut deep into the silver.

With only moments to spare Viona was dragged free

as that huge stalactite of silver and rock splintered down on the spot where she had been. With it came boulders and stones of all sizes, together with clouds of dust. The entire miniature avalanche descended, hazing the view beyond in dust and debris, and making the entire underworld quake dangerously until the disturbance was over.

Then, gradually, the fall subsided and the rumbling ceased. Through the cloud of dust the Amazon looked at the shaken Viona grimly.

"I hope you're satisfied, Viona," she said curtly.

"Just—just about." Viona was breathing hard. "I'm sorry, mother. I didn't intend anything like that, believe me. I saw the opening and it just sort of attracted me."

"In future," Abna said, "never get into anything unless you are quite sure you can get out."

"I won't." Viona looked contrite for a moment, then her eyes brightened again. "But at least I discovered something! There's a huge cavern in there, and it probably leads to the heart of the underworld. Can't we examine it now we've got this far? I don't see why we can't."

"Neither do I," Abna said, reflecting. "We've got this far, Vi, so we may as well finish it. The hole's big enough for us to all get through."

Setting the example, he scrambled through to the cavern beyond, dodging the rocks and boulders that had fallen. In a moment or two the others had joined him.

"So the silver's all above," he said finally, flashing

the beam of his torch. "Yet obviously mined from here. See it there—in dozens of veins. All right—come on."

He led the way forward and the others kept up with him, clambering over rocks, tramping over clear spaces, wandering up acclivities, until they began to wonder just how far this enormous cavern extended.

"From the rock formation," Abna said, studying it as they advanced with torches blazing, "I'd say this world is still a comparatively young one. The geologic strata conforms to our own Earth in the carboniferous period."

"Which means—" Viona began, then she stopped dead at a curious thudding noise somewhere ahead. The odd thing was that the thudding was accompanied by snorts.

"What now?" Abna asked warily, his hand on his protonic gun.

He hadn't long to wait for the answer to his question. Out of the limitless expanses of the underworld, coming presently from total darkness into the range of the torch beams, came the most fantastic animal the four had ever seen—and in their adventures on other worlds they had seen a good few. But this one dwarfed anything.

It moved with cumbersome slowness, which was not surprising considering it must have weighed 100 tons at least. Its enormous height took it nearly to the roof of the stalactited cavern. The eyes of dinner-plate dimensions glared in the torchlight, on either side of a horned snout. The skin was in furrows of armor-gray, and the colossal back sprouted a wealth of needle-pointed barbs, Altogether, a beast of fearsome appearance and from all aspects, a fearsome temper too.

CHAPTER THREE
TRAPPED

Quietly the four stood ready for action, their guns leveled. There was no possible way of escaping the brute: if it attacked they would have to fight for their lives.

Suddenly it sprang into action—and with remarkable speed for a brute so cumbersome. It charged forward with stupendous juggernaut force, growls of fury belching from its deep throat. The quartet stumbled backwards, flying in all directions to escape the juggernaut advance. By inches they missed the monstrous feet, then they swung round and fired their protonic guns.

The beast reared and shrieked as searing fire scorched its armor-hide, but it was by no means severely injured. Eyes glaring, it swung its colossal head to find the source of the irritation.

"Run, to the left," Abna advised quickly. "There's a deep chasm. It might possibly blunder into it."

They did not wait to try further conclusions with the monster, but fled for their lives towards the cleft in the cavern floor, which Abna had indicated. Instantly the monster whirled round—it seemed to have a tail half a mile long—and blundered after them.

"If this doesn't work, we're finished," Viona panted. "Or else we leap into the chasm!"

"Dodge to one side when we reach the edge," Abna retorted—and he did just that when the chasm was reached, the Amazon following him. Viona and Mexone went in the opposite direction and trusted to blind luck.

The ruse worked. The monster was traveling far too fast and was altogether too huge to stop dead when its intended victims weaved away to either side. It plunged clean over the edge of the chasm, slithered, and then with an appalling roar went sailing out into space. The concussion as its 100-ton body struck the base of the chasm seemed to shake the cavern. There was a final despairing, ear-splitting animal shriek and then silence.

Slowly the four retraced their way to each other and gave rather strained glances in the torchlight.

"Nice playmates we've got around here," Abna said, putting his gun hack in its holster "I begin to see now what Doxa meant when he referred to the smaller animals having been destroyed by the larger."

"And we don't know how many more there are of them, or in what variety," the Amazon pointed out. "Our weapons are not powerful enough to have any immediate effect. Do you suppose we ought to return to the *Ultra* for some small-sized atomic bombs? They're our best protection."

Abna reflected. "It seems a pity to go back when we've come this far, but perhaps you're right. Okay, let's go."

So they began the return journey, which as far as giant animals was concerned was entirely uneventful. They did however see a number of the smaller creatures, such as the Asronians used for food. They were docile, very swift little creatures about the size of an earthly lamb, with enormous eyes obviously provided as a means of seeing clearly in the black underworld. Possibly they were sensitive to infrared, or heat radiation. They came and went suddenly as the quartet retraced their way—shy, fleeting creatures whose actual habitat was as yet unknown.

They came at last to the crude hole in silver, and then stopped in startled amazement.

The hole was blocked completely—on the further side!

"Any ideas?" the Amazon asked, grimly, as she slowed to a standstill. "I'll gamble everything I've got that that isn't a natural blockage. In any case there's nothing on the other side that can fall down."

"The thing's deliberate, obviously," Abna responded. "And we don't have to think far to realize that Scind must be responsible. He hasn't been in favor of us ever since he took over.... It means that, although we didn't notice it, we must have been watched when we came down here."

Viona moved forward and inspected the barrier intently; then she glanced up.

"Lucky for Scind and his merry men that we went through this hole, otherwise they'd have had no means of blocking us."

"The hole has obviously been used by them for hunting purposes," Abna mused. "Until we enlarged it.... As for them being lucky in the fact that we came through this hole, they would undoubtedly have found some other way to ditch us. Take our ropes away from the top of the silver chasm, for instance."

The Amazon started. "Great heavens, do you suppose that they have? Those ropes are our only means of getting above."

"Which Scind has obviously realized," Abna said grimly. "Incidentally, when you come to think of it, this hole in its original size would be just big enough for this pygmy race to get through." He held out his hand. "Give me your gun, Mexone. Better see what we can do to break this barrier open."

Mexone handed it over, and Abna only took a moment to reload it. Then he fired it at the barrier. It look three attempts before the mass of rock forming the blockage had been blasted out of existence, evidence enough in itself that, without a proton gun, it would have been impossible to escape.

"Now we'll know the worst," Abna said, pushing his way through to the narrow passage beyond.

The others quickly followed him, hurrying along the short length of narrow cleft. When they came to the point where they had descended, they found them- selves staring at a blank wall of polished silver. The nylon ropes had been withdrawn.

"Now we know what sort of a person we're fighting," Abna said slowly. "To scale this sheer wall is completely impossible. It must be all of 300 feet in height."

For a moment there was silence. The four stared up at the night sky; their first view of it from this fantastic world. They beheld a glittering array of stars in a deep purple sky, sheared off where the edges of the chasm came.

"That's funny," Viona said, and the other looked at her in the torchlight.

"What is?" the Amazon inquired.

"I'll swear I'm not seeing things," Viona continued, staring above. "A moment ago I was looking at a triangular group of stars up there. Now they've gone! They went suddenly, just as though something had come in between. But there are no clouds or anything."

Abna looked above long and earnestly. "No, you're not seeing things," he answered at length. "I noticed that triangular group of stars.... And now they've gone!"

"But three stars couldn't just vanish like that!" Viona protested.

"They could if a machine dictated a different probability for them. Just the same as a different probability was dictated for Doxa when he was supposedly transported to 'Paradise'."

"You mean the—machine?" the Amazon asked sharply.

"Why not? If it can reach things on this planet, there

is nothing to prevent it reaching far out into space. There's going to be real trouble before long. We must find that machine."

This time the Amazon did not attempt to argue him out of it, She had had experience before of Abna's uncanny prescience.

"There's no way out of here," he said, looking about him. "Scind has managed to seal us up very effectually, so our only hope is to press on with what weapons we've got. Maybe we'll find a way out by going into the underworld; there surely must be more than one way in from the surface. We'll go back again through the hole in the silver wall."

So the second excursion into the depths began, Abna and the others always on the lookout for a possible way out to the surface—but none presented itself. Perhaps, even, all the entrances to the underworld were made by way of the chasm.... Once only did they stop for a while, and that was when the Amazon made a lightning killing with her bare hands of one of the smaller animals. It necessitated a pause for a much-needed meal washed down by restorative drinks from the flasks they had with them. What time it was by now they had no idea, but any feeling of tiredness was practically impossible with their immense strength and the ever-present feeling of exhilaration.

Then on their way again, pausing at length when they came to the chasm into which the 100-ton monster had blindly plunged.

"What now? The Amazon asked. "We're back to our

original turning point."

"This chasm seems to stretch for a good distance, and we certainly can't descend into it," Abna responded. "Let's go to the left and see what happens."

They did so, carrying on for perhaps three miles and beginning to think they were on a useless journey—when suddenly Mexone gave a cry.

"Look ahead there! A sort of bridge!"

He was right. The range of the lamps extended just far enough to reveal a gleaming bar projecting right across the chasm. Upon reaching it, it proved to be a single block of silver, about eighteen inches wide and a foot thick. It extended right across the chasm, but was lost to sight in darkness where it touched the other side. For a moment the four lost themselves in speculations as to how much such a bar might be worth in the Earth money market.

"Plainly this has been put here deliberately lo act as a bridge," Abna said. "Which makes it look as though our childlike friends have been farther into these depths than we ever imagined. Where it leads to—beyond the other side of the chasm—we don't know. So here goes toward finding out."

He tested the silver bridge carefully, was immediately satisfied that it was quite secure, and then prepared to walk across it. He did so with complete fearlessness, unable to see the bottom of the chasm he was crossing, or for that matter to either side of him. Only this one gleaming ribbon extending into dark—

But not for long. The beams of his head torch presently picked up the chasm's other side and in a moment or two he had set foot safely on solid ground again. Then he waited as first the Amazon, then Viona and Mexone, came across and joined him.

An hour passed as the four wandered through interminable galleries of rock across plains of rocks shot through with silver, along tunnels, up acclivities, along rimrocks, through volcanic fissures—until at last even the spurious high spirits created by the mysterious radiation began to flag a little and brought their wanderings to a halt. Sleep was decided upon, one of them to remain on watch—in turn—in case anything untoward developed.

Nothing did, throughout the watch of each one then left on guard. Altogether, some eight hours passed spent in sleeping, then a meal was made of the remains of the slain animal they had brought with them, and the advances resumed.

It looked like being a boring repetition of what they had already experienced—at least to begin with. Then when they had been on their way perhaps an hour, Abna, in the lead, came to a sudden halt. The others, only a little behind, caught up with him and stood staring from a high ledge of rock down into a kind of crater. In that moment they realized that their search was ended.

Before and below them perhaps twenty feet down in the cleared region of the crater floor, was the mysterious something that they had been seeking. Their lamps were reflected back from its silver metal sides.

"That must be it," Abna said at length, taking a deep breath. "Or at any rate part of it."

They continued to view it from a distance. Carefully turning their lamps, they could see that the machine was wired into the floor of the crater by immensely thick cables, but there was no evidence of where the cables went to. They simply snaked into the rocks and embedded themselves. There was no sign of a controlling switchboard.

In height the machine stood an approximate fifteen feet, and was perhaps five feet wide. It most resembled an old-fashioned kind of silver helmet, or pointed bell, with the wide base to the ground. Whatever controls there were—except for a projecting boxlike affair on one side—were evidently within the cowling. On the face of it, the thing looked harmless. That it was not was evident by the greatly increased sense of elation-inducing waves that the quartet could now sense.

"How does the thing work with nobody lo look after it?" Mexone asked at length, logically enough.

Abna shook his head. "Can't tell you that until we've examined it at close quarters. We'd better go and—"

The rest of Abna's words were drowned by a sudden, ground-shaking roar. Startled, the quartet swung around and saw that another monster—of a different type this time—had come up in their rear with surprising silence. Now it was in the midst of studying them, its red-rimmed dinner-plate eyes filled with a vicious hatred.

"Here we go again," Abna muttered grimly, and felt

for a ray gun that he no longer possessed. This being so, he stood a little to the rear of the others as they tugged out their weapons and prepared to defend themselves.

"I'm beginning to get an idea about these monsters," Viona said, watching the beast warily. "I begin to think they're left to roam to deal with any strangers who prowl around the machine. As for the little people, I can't imagine how they manage."

The others did not answer: they were too intent on wondering what was going to happen next. So while the beast weighed them up, they, too, studied it.... It was not as big as its predecessor, and is far as the four could determine, it had some kinship with the earthly iguanodon, as far as structure was concerned, but not in regard to temperament, since it was obviously a killer.

With a bellowing roar it thundered forward, and fast though they traveled, Viona and Mexone were no match for the terrific speed of the creature with its outthrust neck. Within seconds the head flashed downwards, and at the identical moment, looking over her shoulder, Viona stumbled and fell flat on her face. This inadvertence saved her—but Mexone was not so lucky.

Things happened so fast the Amazon and Abna could only stare in horrified amazement as Mexone was swept from his feet, those mighty jaws closing about his waist. Immediately he was whirled helplessly into the air, struggling savagely to fire his ray gun. In a moment or so he succeeded, driving the pencil of fire straight into the creature's right eye, the only vulnerable spot he could find in his extremity.

The creature howled with appalling fury as the sight of its eye was instantly destroyed. Maddened with pain, it hurtled forward with greater energy than before, charging straight toward the distant wall of the cavern. Mexone had time to marvel that those monstrous jaws had not crushed him, but up to now they were merely holding him in a vice-like grip. Maybe the monster's idea was to toy with him before killing him, as a cat might play with a mouse.

"After him!" the Amazon shouted, firing at the retreating ironclad. "Viona! Quickly!"

Viona did not need any telling. She was on her feet again, chasing after the monster and firing her proton gun savagely as she moved. Unless the brute were headed off, in its maddened state it would crash straight into the farther cavern wall, with disastrous results to Mexone. He for his part, realizing he was still alive and uninjured, was aiming his gun for a second attack—this time on the other eye of the giant.

But suddenly there was a change, so complete and startling that it stopped the Amazon, Viona, and weaponless Abna in their tracks. They felt a sudden constriction in the atmosphere, a strange tautening of the nerves that made movement almost impossible for a second or two. At the same time the monster gave an appalling howl and dropped Mexone heavily from its jaws. Nor was that the finish—for abruptly the monster, and the cavern wall behind it, misted mysteriously and ceased to be. There remained a huge hole in the rock and no trace whatever of the beast. Low down on the floor, some distance from the disturbance, Mexone was slowing picking himself up.

"What's happened?" Viona gasped, looking back in amazement.

The Amazon and Abna slowly felt life surge back into them. They did not answer Viona immediately for the simple reason that they were staring ahead of them at an enormous opening of night, filled with coldly winking stars.

"The outside!" the Amazon whispered at last. "Thank heaven for that!"

There was no doubt but what she was right. Mexone, now on his feet, completely dazed by the suddenness of everything, turned as Viona came up to him anxiously.

"All right?" she inquired quickly.

"Yes, I'm okay." Mexone glanced at her. "But what happened? Where's the monster gone? How did this huge exit to the outer world get here?"

"The machine," Abna said, arriving with the Amazon. "That's the answer. It's a repetition of what happened to Doxa and his transport to Paradise. This machine must have emitted one of its deeper probability waves and it happened—most fortunately—to strike the monster and the rock wall. The result was that both vanished as they yielded to a new probability."

Viona and Mexone nodded slowly, absorbing the amazing fact. They were not so quick to appreciate the scientific implications as the older pair.

"Perhaps," the Amazon said, after a moment or two,

"much of this underworld has been blasted into emptiness by the effect of these probability waves. I could hardly see a race of men, however skilled scientifically, hollowing out a planet as thoroughly as this one.... Not that it matters: just a thought. The intriguing part is that we have a way out, and we also know that this machine down in the crater here is functioning. What do we do next, Abna? Examine the machine?"

"We return to the *Ultra*," Abna replied decisively. "We want to find out how we stand with Scind. He will probably he quite surprised to see us still alive. We'll leave him to guess how we got out of the underworld. Come!"

So the four emerged into the open and stood for a moment surveying the night sky. Viona looked up quizzically at the unfamiliar constellations.

"One thing I don't understand," she said. "If that was a probability wave, and it has gone out into space, why is it that a star—or stars—in direct line with it overhead, haven't disappeared?"

"The answer is the speed of light," Abna replied, switching off his head-torch. "The nearest stars to us must be many light-years away. Since light moves at 186,000 miles a second, it will be years before the wave reaches any of those stars and extinguishes it. Those we saw wink out earlier were obviously the victims of a much earlier wave."

The Amazon looked over the silver plain, faintly reflective in the starlight. A cool, thin wind was blowing across it.

"Better make for the *Ultra*," she decided. "Which way is it, Abna?"

He looked at his compass, studying the luminous needle. "That way," he said at length, pointing. "We ought to make it easily enough, but there's one big snag in the way. The chasm, down which we originally descended. Now we'll come to it from the other side, and we haven't got ropes."

"Only one thing to do," Viona said after a momentary silence. "When we come to the chasm we'll have to go along it until we find a place where it ends or, failing that, a point where it narrows enough to jump it. Certainly we're not going back into the underworld when we've found the way out—at least not until we've got proper provisions and weapons. Agreed?"

"Agreed," the Amazon said. "Let's be on our way."

"We must have slept a good deal longer than we thought," Abna commented. "Another day seems to have slipped past while we've been in the underworld. All to the good. Sunlight on this planet is a little too forceful to be pleasant."

CHAPTER FOUR
SCIND'S TREACHERY

The journey through the night was monotonous and uneventful, but at least the pace at which the four moved saved them from feeling any sense of cold as the thin, unpleasant wind blew about them. Considering the tremendous heat of the day, it was surprising how cold was the night, until they came to reflect that the absence of cloud-cover permitted the day heat to radiate swiftly from the surface.

In all, it took them an hour and a half to reach the chasm again, a surprisingly short time considering how long they had been wandering in the underworld. Once they gained it, they stood looking into its depths—then to left and right as it extended in a black line under the stars.

"Right or left?" the Amazon asked, and Abna looked at his compass once more.

"From the look of this, it's nearer to our right than our left—the *Ultra*, I mean. So we'd better take right."

They moved on again, watching the chasm for some sign of it narrowing, or becoming less in depth, but no such thing happened. They were becoming weary now—not so much from physical fatigue as from monotony, and were just on the point of accepting the fact that perhaps the chasm did go right around the planet, when Viona—a little in the lead—gave a sudden cry and pointed.

"Look! Another of those bridges!"

At present the bridge was only visible in the distance as a straight, glittering line in the starlight. The quartet wasted no time in reaching it and found that it was indeed another of those silver bars bridging the depths. Promptly Abna went down on his knees and examined it.

"Why do you do that each time?" the Amazon asked, puzzled.

"Why? Because I don't trust Scind and his merry men. Since they're so anxious to get rid of us, I wouldn't put it past them to half-saw one of these silver bridges through and leave us to find out the fact when we're halfway over.... However, this one seems to be all right, so we can cross."

To prove his own words he walked across and stood waiting on the other side. The Amazon followed him, then Viona and Mexone. By the time Mexone had arrived so also had daylight, with a suddenness that was startling. One moment it was deep night and the next the blinding magnesium sun was blazing just above the horizon and commencing its relentless climb into the heavens.

"I don't know whether it's a help or a hindrance," Abna said, narrowing his eyes in the glare. "Either way we might as well continue. When we finally reach the *Ultra* we can take a rest."

So again they went forward, and within another hour they had come to the outermost dwellings of the 'settlement' occupied by Scind and his colleagues. The men and women were up and astir, but they bestowed no more than a passing interest on the four grim-faced travelers who strode through their midst. The real surprise came when they reached Scind's abode, just as Scind himself was about to leave on some errand or other. As he saw the four bearing down upon him, he just stared incredulously.

"Greetings, travelers!" he exclaimed, recovering himself rapidly. "I trust you had a worthwhile exploration?"

"Very," the Amazon said, eyeing him levelly.

"What's the idea, Scind?" Abna asked bluntly. "Why did you have to have us followed, and remove the ropes from the chasm? That was our only way of getting out of the underworld—and you knew it."

"I—I had to!" the little man blustered. "Or haven't you realized that you're not welcome here? You say you want to help us, yet you want to destroy the machine which takes us to Paradise. It was better that I try to stop you."

The Amazon gave a puzzled smile, such as a parent indulging an obstinate child.

"Are you such a fool, Scind, as to believe this nonsense about Paradise?" Abna demanded. "Don't you know what transportation really means? It doesn't mean Paradise. It means transference into something you never dreamed of, a complete reorganization of body and mind!"

Abna was wasting his time, and Scind's face clearly showed it.

"You have no right to come here, telling us what we should and shouldn't do! Leave us alone! Go away! Let us work out our destiny in our own way."

"If it were only your own destiny, we would comply," Abna answered. "But we have strong reasons for believing that your ancestors have done something which places the whole Universe in jeopardy. For that reason we shall remain here and examine this mysterious machine which is supposed to transport you to Paradise."

"We are working for your own good," the Amazon insisted. "We realize that you are a race of people without scientific knowledge, or even the intelligence to grapple with a thing like this. We are doing our best to save you from yourselves."

With that the Amazon turned away, and Abna, Mexone, and Viona caught up with her as she strode toward the *Ultra*.

"Tell you one thing, Vi," Abna said, falling into step beside her. "The more I see of this fellow Scind the more I think he's mad. Maybe radiation has affected him in a way different from the others."

"Could be," the Amazon admitted. "Either that or else he has delusions of grandeur because he happens to possess the knack of ruling the rest of the people."

"It's obvious," Abna continued, "that they know where this machine is and have been led to regard it more as a benefit than an evil. They, therefore, don't take kindly to the idea of our destroying it—as witness the effort to trap us in the underworld."

The Amazon shrugged. "They think and act like children, and as such must be treated. Sometimes I feel the urge to treat them like grown-ups, particularly Scind—then I force myself to remember that they're quite sincere in what they're doing."

"Have to see how they react," Abna decided. "I've the feeling we haven't finished with Scind by any means."

The Amazon passed no further comment. Viona and Mexone did not comment either; so mainly in silence the *Ultra* was regained. Immediately the Amazon made a check of the controls and power plant, then she relaxed a trifle.

"At least they've done no damage here," she said, and swung the airlock shut. "Best thing we can do is have a meal and a rest, then begin again. Agreed?"

They nodded, and Viona, whose job it was, began the preparation of a meal, helped by Mexone.

* * * * * * *

"Sometimes," Mexone said when the meal was finished, "I honestly wonder why we spend our time getting into trouble and trying to help other people on alien worlds. It would be a good deal more comfortable to just cruise around as we wish and not keep sticking out our chins."

"It would be more comfortable," the Amazon agreed, "but it would also be decidedly selfish. We believe that we have unusual gifts, some natural and some acquired. No gift can flourish if one keeps it to oneself—no matter what discomfort it entailed, we believe we should help the not-so-gifted. That is the whole purpose of the Cosmic Crusaders. Being comparatively new to our little group, you haven't quite absorbed it yet.... Right, Abna?"

"Right," Abna agreed absently; then he roused himself to alertness and made an announcement.

"We'll each of us have a sleep, one to remain on guard, and—"

"On guard?" the Amazon repeated. "But why? Nobody can do a thing from the outside of this machine: it's invincible. Certainly Scind and his little boys can't do anything."

"Very well," Abna shrugged. "We'll each of us sleep and then tackle whatever difficulties there are when we awake."

The decision arrived at, it was put into practice, and all the exhilaration waves emanated from the mystery machine could not prevent the four realizing how dog-tired they really were. They slept deeply, to awaken again ready for action as the blinding sun was lowering to the horizon.

There followed a further meal, a packing of adequate provisions, and a check-over of arms and ammunition, then Abna looked at each of the three faces in turn.

"I realize," he said quietly, "that none of you really appreciate how vital this particular excursion is. You think we are just going to examine a machine—but it is much more than that. I still believe that the whole universe may be threatened by this effort to alter electronic probability laws, and for that reason the threat must be removed."

"Whatever the consequences, we'll have to risk them," the Amazon said. "Let's get started and see what happens."

Abna turned to the switchboard and depressed the airlock control. The airlock door began to move inwards silently, hut hardly had it swung a quarter of its length before child-people from outside hurtled into the control room, men and women both, shouting to each other in their own queer language.

"Look out!" Mexone cried, making a grab at his gun and thrusting Viona behind him.

"Everybody in the tribe, I should think—" the Amazon started to say.

The child-people surged forward in dozens and hundreds, taking full advantage of the surprise they had sprung. Before Abna had time to turn from the switch panel, he found himself surrounded, struggling desperately, and his great height certainly did nothing to save him from their swarming numbers. Clawing desperately at the little folk as they crawled tenaciously up his great form, he found himself pulled sideways, and at last crashed to the floor.

So it was with the Amazon, Viona, and Mexone.

Though they made an effort to tug out their weapons, they were pulled over and slammed on their backs before they could do a thing. The sheer weight of numbers, and the relentless persistency of the small enemy, did the trick. Rope came next—their own nylon cords which they had used in the chasm—and the four found themselves securely fastened with their hands tethered with excruciating tightness behind their backs.

Not until they were certain that the quartet was helpless, did the little folk move back slightly to permit Scind himself to come forward. He did so with the air of an insolent child, grinning widely with triumph.

"I believe, my friends, that your sole object in being on this planet is to investigate the machine in our underworld? I have considered that fact carefully—but I have also considered that you might learn a good deal more if you studied it at very close quarters."

None of the four said anything. The Amazon wrestled mightily with the tough nylon cord, but since it was in four thicknesses even she was beaten…so far. She gave Abna a grim look and he raised an eyebrow. It seemed to say 'I told you so!' with exquisite eloquence.

"Why don't you stop heating around the bush?" the Amazon demanded of Scind. "Why don't you realize that everything we're doing is calculated lo help you? If you harm us, it will only be the worse for yourselves in the long run."

Just for a moment a vague look of fear crossed Scind's face, but it went almost as quickly. He drew himself up.

"I do not believe in your so-called superior intellect, and neither do my followers. We have decided to be rid of you, and in the manner most befitting.… Away with them!" he added curtly, motioning with his hands.

There was nothing more to be said. Despite their savage struggles, the four were lifted by the little people and borne outside, in much the same manner as Gulliver by the Lilliputians. They were carried face upwards, on the creatures' shoulders, forced to stare at the glaring cobalt of the evening sky as they were carried across the silver plain and presently beyond the habitation of the 'settlement.'

When the chasm was reached, a halt was called, and the four were laid on the ground, wondering grimly what was going to happen next. Under Scind's directions the four each had a rope fastened to their existing bonds, and then were pushed unceremoniously over the chasm edge. They fell with unnerving speed until the ropes drew light, then the rest of the drop they were lowered carefully, the little people straining hard as they took the weight. Thus the four eventually found themselves in the chasm bottom, still unable to release themselves, and the little folks came swarming down the ropes in their dozens as a few of their followers remained at the top to provide an anchorage.

"Descending into this chasm is nothing new to us," Scind observed, coming over to where the four lay, and brandishing an ancient type of oil-fed torch. "We come down often to slay animals. You evidently found our inlet hole in the wall. We did not make it any larger in case giant animals should escape. You yourselves enlarged it considerably, but not enough to be a menace.… Incidentally, this chasm which encircles the planet is intended to keep monsters imprisoned."

"How did you make such a chasm?" Abna asked in surprise.

"There are some instruments still existing from our ancestors' times—one of them a mechanical borer. That is how we made the chasm, and the hole into the underworld."

Evidently Scind considered he had given enough information, for he signaled sharply to his followers, and once again transportation began—along the corridor, through the hole, and into the depths of the now familiar underworld. The procession was a queer one, with the makeshift torches, the shadows dancing weirdly on the rock and silver walls. Abna at least wondered what would happen if one of the giant monsters or spiders came on the scene, but nothing occurred and the uncomfortable journey continued.

Not once did the army of little people pause in their onward journey. In the main they talked among themselves, all except those who were the actual bearers. They took their job seriously and carried their captives over every conceivable obstacle, even including the silver bridge over the underground chasm, in the depths of which lay the slain monster of the earlier exploration. Sure-footed, they transported the quartet across the bridge without so much as a pause—then on again over the wearying, monotonous journey until at last they were descending the crater side, on the floor of which was the machine.

Stiff and cramped from the constriction of their ropes, the four were set down on the crater floor, looking up at the little people surging around them — then presently at Scind as he came to the fore, holding his queer torch.

"This is the journey's end, my friends," he remarked, obviously enough. "Behind you is the machine which you are so interested in. Sooner or later it will emit one of its strange transportations to Paradise, and you will be able to follow the process thoroughly. More than that I do not need to say.... Except that there is a second alternative."

"And what's that?" the Amazon snapped.

"As you will know, this region is not entirely devoid of giant monsters. One of them may find you before the machine operates. They cannot possibly damage the machine, but they can certainly attack and kill you." Scind shrugged. "That is left to chance. If the machine does not rid us of you, then the monsters will—"

Scind broke off suddenly as one of his followers, bearing a torch, came hurrying forward. He gave some information in the chattering tongue of his own language and Scind's harsh face darkened a trifle. Abruptly, he turned again to the quartet.

"I have just been informed that there is a very big hole in the cavern wall not far from here, my friends. Apparently it is so big that you yourselves could not have created it. That leaves only the machine as the cause, and it also explains how you escaped from the underworld."

"Quite correct," Abna assented. "And once we escape from these ropes, we'll be free again and escape the same way. You can be sure of that, Scind."

Scind smiled cynically. "I think not. I admit your strength, but you will never have the power to break the bonds we shall fasten about you."

Thereupon he gave his usual signal and the little men and women swarmed to obey his order. Evidently they knew what to do, for they lifted the quartet one by one and leaned them against the four sides of the machine. Then rope and wire were added to their tight nylon cords, knotted and looped around the projections of the machine until not one of them could move a muscle. When the job was done, Scind swaggered around the machine, surveying each of his captives in turn, finally coming to a halt again as he faced Abna.

"I have deliberately waited for this moment," Scind said grimly. "I have already made it clear to you that we do not want you here, interfering with our affairs. You have ignored my warning. Therefore, I think it necessary to show you that I can implement my warnings with force."

Scind pulled something that he had been carrying on his back. Surprisingly, it proved to he a small whip with two tails, each weighted with a top of silver. His next words seemed to set the seal on the possibility of madness.

"Before there was any particular order among our numbers, before you and your three colleagues came from the outer spaces and conferred language upon us, I had my own way of dealing with fractious members of the community."

"A tin pot dictator with a little whip," the Amazon said. "You make it very clear."

"I intend to make it clearer," Scind said, and on the last word his whip lashed forward and the twin tails struck the Amazon down the face with savage force. She closed her eyes and winced as blood was drawn.

Immediately—and rather surprisingly—seven men and women in the group dashed forward to restrain Scind, only to receive the lash themselves and go stumbling backwards—but at least it showed what their real reactions were to the little madman controlling them. He stood challengingly, feet apart, waiting for the next. The people quieted, watching him in awe and not a little fear, their eyes straying to the Amazon, blood trickling down her face.

Though he could not see what was going on by reason of his position, Abna struggled mightily to free himself. The nylon cord pulled to the limit, but it was proof even against his iron muscles. Finally, breathing hard, he desisted.

"I hope," Scind remarked, replacing the whip on his back, "that you now understand the situation. Later I shall deal with these people of mine who dared to try to restrain me."

He turned away and began to issue orders to his

people. Slowly the gathering began to break up and returned up the crater side. After a while there came harsh, unintelligible shouts from the distance and the sound of heavy rocks being levered reverberatingly into position.

"At least," Abna said, still straining at his bonds, "we have had a perfect insight into Scind's character. As we thought, it isn't the little people in general who are against us so much as Scind himself. It's a pity Doxa was snatched away when he was. With him as ruler we might have talked sense into these folks."

"Possibly," the Amazon admitted. "If we were not dealing with a madman who obviously doesn't clearly know what he's doing, I'd leave nothing unturned to find Scind and eliminate him. As it is, I shan't. We've more imperative things to do."

She said no more but proceeded to throw every ounce of her strength into an effort to break free. The muscles rolled beneath her tawny skin, and her face—cut and blood-streaked—was set in a mask of unrelenting strain. Time and again she exerted her superhuman power to the utmost, and so did Abna.

And at last there was a result. One strand of the nylon rope about the Amazon's arms gave way. She did not instantly redouble her efforts: instead she gave a grim smile and completely relaxed for a few moments.

"One gone!" Abna said suddenly in triumph. "If we work on it long enough we'll do it—or at least I will. If one rope will snap, the others will."

"One of mine has also gone!" the Amazon retorted.

"So you are not alone in your glory!"

Abna smiled faintly. It was typical of the Amazon, despite the predicament, to extract supreme satisfaction from matching her strength against his. Perhaps even, on this occasion, it was a good thing they had to. It made the pair of them exert themselves to the limit—and even a bit beyond that—in an effort to achieve muscular victory.

Furiously, Abna strained and twisted—then something happened. Abna found himself careening head over heels in the void. The stars and nebulae were blazing around him and there was no trace of a solid world anywhere. Abna realized that his physical body was extending into wraith-like consistency, with the planet Tuca a brightly gleaming speck in infinity. On the other hand, his intelligence lived on.

Uncertainly and wonderingly he looked into a new space, a space wherein all the probabilities of electronic law were strangely altered, where death was life, where retrogression meant progress, where love perhaps meant hate. A complete and stunning inversion of all so-called natural laws.

Just as quickly the vision shut down and Abna knew that he was on the point of death. Nothing could save him from that except his mind—that superb scientific mind, which was the absolute master of metaphysics. With every vestige of his mentality, he threw himself against the strangling suggestion that death was inevitable....

CHAPTER FIVE
THE TRANSITION OF ABNA

With a last tremendous effort the Amazon broke the nylon cords that were pinning her arms, and from then on the rest of the struggle was easy. By dint of twisting and maneuvering, she succeeded in reaching the proton gun in her belt. It was already on the smallest nozzle from previous use, so the biting ray of energy made short work of the remaining pieces of wire holding her body to the machine.

Instantly she hurried around in triumph to Abna, and then paused in dumbfounded amazement. She had heard nothing, though she had wondered why his comments had suddenly ceased. Now she beheld no trace of him. Not a wire, not a rope.... Amazed, she turned slowly and looked around her. Almost immediately she beheld a gaping hole in the cavern roof, which formed itself into a tunnel with a tiny spot of daylight hanging like a star at the far end.

"The machine—probability—" she whispered. "And it took Abna with it...."

For several moments she stood trying to absorb the grim situation. Still half mechanically, she went around to where Viona was struggling and cut her loose. When she had done the same for Mexone, she returned to the spot where Abna had been and the two younger ones joined her.

"But what's happened?" Viona asked, horrified. "I didn't hear anything, Where's father gone?"

"Pretty obvious, isn't it?" the Amazon demanded. "The machine has emitted another probability wave in a fixed direction. Your father must have been in direct line with it."

"I can't—and won't—believe it!" Viona declared passionately. "Father had too fine a mind to he caught like that—"

"It's no question of being caught!" The Amazon was irritable with ill-concealed grief. "The very suddenness of it would be enough. Your father just wouldn't have had time to grapple with the situation."

The Amazon fell silent, her mood slowly changing. After a moment or too she clenched her fists.

"We were prepared to do everything possible to help the people on this planet, and how are we rewarded? By treachery and murder!" Her eyes blazed suddenly. "Not by all the people, I admit, but certainly by Scind." She felt the wheels on her face slowly. "He alone is responsible for the death of your father! He is a killer, and there's no escaping the fact."

"What do we do about the machine?" Mexone asked, seeking to change the subject, and the mood.

"I'm not concerned about it any more. I'm only concerned with the fact that Abna is dead and we know who caused it. Come! Let us see what we can do toward blasting the rocks in the cavern wall. This other tunnel is too high up to be of any advantage."

She turned purposefully from the machine to the crater side and then paused and pressed finger and thumb to her eyes. For a moment she thought she was suffering from delusions—until Mexone and Viona both gave cries of amazement.

"There's something coming out of the air!"

The Amazon waited, staring fixedly with Viona and Mexone on either side of her. As yet the apparition had no determinate shape. It was a 'something' near the machine, through which the crater side was visible, but as the seconds passed it took on a certain solidity.

"It's—it's father!" Viona shouted hoarsely, and made to run forward, but the Amazon snatched her back.

"Wait! Don't disturb his concentration!"

Viona did as she was told, Mexone standing beside her. The Amazon relinquished her grip and gazed immovably at the slowly merging figure. Before long it became obvious that it was indeed Abna, his hands clenched at his sides and his head bowed as with tremendous effort. So, at length, he became completely solid, and with that he relaxed.

"Abna!" the Amazon cried, hurrying forward. "Thank heaven for that!"

For a moment the Amazon so far forgot her cold, scientific detachment as to hurry into Abna's embrace. He gripped her shoulders firmly, and Viona's, too— then looked at them both.

"So you got free?" he asked quietly.

"Yes—I broke free," the Amazon acknowledged, detaching herself. "But what happened to you? It was a probability wave, wasn't it?"

"Just that," he agreed. "One moment I was struggling to smash the ropes—and the next I was in infinity." A faraway look came into his eyes. "I was nearly dead, but I had the good sense to realize the fact. My body had reached the limit of attenuation. It was a case of mind over matter—which would prove the stronger force. You know my metaphysical powers when I choose to use them. By the greatest effort I have ever made in my life, I forced myself back against the probability waves to the starting point, and so vanquished material law. And here I am."

"Knowing your powers metaphysically, it doesn't surprise me," the Amazon responded. "But none of this alters the fact that one person alone is responsible for it all. Scind! I think I should go right now and find him. We were just about to break open the cavern wall where they have rocked it up."

"I notice the probability wave which encompassed me left a sizeable tunnel in the roof," Abna commented, looking up at it.

"Yes," the Amazon assented briefly, examining her proton gun. "But we've got a job to do—if you feel up to it, Abna?"

"It was a wonderful sight," he went on absently, apparently hardly hearing the Amazon. "A new space, which contains an inversion of everything as we know it. Backwards must be interpreted as forwards: love must mean hate. Everything the reverse of what we know. A fascinating region, this never-never land of electronic probability gone mad. A fair picture, I'd say, of how the universe will look if this machine is allowed to have full sway. At the moment only a portion of the universe is affected, and it was given to me to glimpse it.... But for the urgency of my physical condition, I would have stayed much longer."

The Amazon nodded and prepared to move on, gun in hand—but Abna reached out and detained her.

"That can wait," he said. "I know your feelings, but does that matter so much now I've come back? Kill Scind, and you lose the confidence of the people. They believe we're trying to help them, which we are. The murder of Scind would make them think things. In any event, we have much more important things to attend to."

The Amazon hesitated, until she had analyzed the position. Only then did she re-holster her proton gun and follow Abna, Mexone, and Viona across to the machine. At a little distance from it, Abna stopped and surveyed.

"The only possible way into it seems to be by the boxlike affair on the side," he said at length. "Better see how it unfastens."

With that, Abna strode forward and looked at the boxlike protuberance more closely. The first thing that became obvious was that it was merely attached by a slot process on to a series of bolts. Since the whole issue was silver, there was no evidence of corrosion.

"Obviously just a protective cover," Abna said, and lifted it off, to reveal an intricate mesh of slowly moving mechanism like the inside of a complicated clock.

"Has it occurred to you that any moment any one of us may be swept into infinity—as you were?" Mexone asked. "And we shan't have the same capacity as you to find the way back."

Abna nodded slowly. "I'm aware of the danger, but that is just one of those things that we shall have to risk. One thing I do know: we want close photoprints of this machinery as we take it apart."

The Amazon looked surprised. "Might I ask why?"

"Tell you later. It's an idea I've got."

He took a small micro-camera from his instrument belt, fixed the automatic focusing button, and pressed the switch. There was the evanescent flare of the atomic floodlight and the first picture was taken. But Abna was not satisfied until he had taken at least six shots from differing angles, then he put the camera hack in his belt.

"Souvenirs?" the Amazon inquired dryly, and Abna smiled.

"You might call it that. I'll explain later on. Now to try dismantling."

He studied the moving intricacy attentively, noting the movement of each delicate part, and they were legion, with the whole mass of complication centering on a broad spindle which was spinning effortlessly and connected somewhere to the inside of the machine.

"Suppose," the Amazon said dubiously, "that dismantling even a part of the machine causes it to blow up?"

"The danger is considerable, and there's no sense in denying it," Abna said. "But if we act logically, I see no reason to expect trouble. This external unit is plainly not of any great importance. It fulfils somewhat the same function as the hands of a watch—namely, it shows the mechanism as a whole is working. What we've got to do is find a way inside the machine itself."

For a while, this presented a decided problem. At first sight the machine seemed to be made in one piece, until careful thought revealed the impossibility of such a thing. Somewhere there must be a way in. There was. It finally became evident as a hair-thin line down the center of each of the four sides.

"The cowling sheets simply fit into one another, on the style of tongue-and-groove boarding," Abna decided. "The job is such a masterpiece of engineering you can hardly see the dividing line. Okay—you take one half, Vi, and I'll take the other, and we'll see what happens."

They stationed themselves at opposite corners of the panel they had selected, and pulled with all their strength. The effect was surprising. The panel parted effortlessly down the middle and the two halves swung aside smoothly on hinges, on a principle no more complicated than a pair of well-made cupboard doors.

"Good!" Abna declared in satisfaction, staring at the wealth of circuits, wiring, and coils now revealed. "Do the same with the other sides and the whole machine is open to us."

Dealing with the other three sides presented no complications. Viona and Mexone tugged them apart between them and within ten minutes, the doors neatly hinged and folded back to the corners, the whole machine lay exposed, a complete masterpiece of scientific engineering.

Time and again Abna's camera flared and clicked; then when he was done he stood surveying from various angles, the Amazon by his side.

"Any suggestions?" he asked her presently.

"As far as dismantling is concerned, none at all. I've been trying to puzzle out what kind of power it uses, and it seems as though it must be planetary. That's the only power which lasts as long as the planet itself."

Abna nodded. "I think you're right, as is evidenced by these wires going into the ground. They are doubtless connected up to various portions of the planet. The planet itself provides the power, since in its constant spinning it is in effect an electrical armature, spinning between poles. We've come across such means of supplying power before, and I think this is merely a repetition of it."

"Which makes the matter of destroying it comparatively simple," Viona commented. "All we have to do is destroy the main power wires, and the thing's done."

"I wonder?" Abna mused. "If we cut one of the wires we will have a tremendous overload on the remaining three, which may cause just anything to happen. There are four wires, and destruction of them should be done simultaneously—which is possible with four of us working in synchronism.... On the other hand, destruction of the power wires doesn't mean the machine is no longer a menace. Wires can he repaired—and probably would be."

"By Scind and his merry men?" Mexone asked doubtfully. "I doubt it! I should hardly give them credit for being able to tie a knot in a piece of string."

"Never underestimate your enemy," Abna said grimly. "They have quite a lot of intelligence, these people, hut they don't use it much. This machine means everything to Scind; he believes with an almost pagan faith that the machine really means transport to Paradise. It is also a useful weapon to hold as a threat against fractious members of the community. He can do with them as he did with ns—tie them to the machine. Probably the very threat of him doing so will be enough for him to secure his ends. No, all things considered, cutting off the power and leaving the machine is not the answer."

"Definitely not," the Amazon said, thinking.

Abna shrugged. "Which leaves only one solution. This machine must be taken to pieces, and each piece must be thoroughly and methodically destroyed as we progress. Finally we shall reach the power wires themselves, but since they'll be supplying power to an empty casing, it won't matter much. At least the power will be confined within the insulated area of the casing and won't cause us any trouble."

The others nodded, following as usual his leadership. He became silent for a while, considering, and then continued:

"The centerpiece of this instrument is plainly mathematical in basis. See this bank of automatic figure keys? From those it may be possible to tell what is eventually intended for this machine. If not that, then at least we may be able to tell how the linking up is arranged. You'd better help me on this problem, Vi. We'd better work it out before we start dismantling."

The Amazon nodded, tugging a notebook from her belt. Abna did likewise and together they began to figure industriously. From the setting of the figures it was possible to work out in advanced mathematics what course the machine would automatically follow, but so profound were the calculations involved and so intricate the equations, it was a good two hours before either of them reached a logical conclusion—two hours in which Viona and Mexone could only stand idly by and await results.

"It looks," the Amazon said at last, "as though your original fears concerning this machine were well-founded. According to my reckoning, its ultimate mathematical effort will be the entire dissolution of the universe."

"How long have we got before—things happen?" Viona asked.

"Not long," Abna told her. "A matter of days. My anxiety over this machine was not misplaced. I had an intuition all along that there was very real danger, but perhaps we've caught it in time."

"Why 'perhaps'?" Viona asked in surprise. "We have, have we not?"

"In a matter as complicated as this, I'm none too sure," the Amazon replied, glancing up. "As I see it, the destruction of the mathematical matrix of this machine can only be done in four stages—the removal of four connecting pins which link up the whole mass. Is that right, Abna?"

"Right," he agreed, and moved more closely to the machine. Then motioning inside it, he continued: "You can see the four pins for yourselves. There— those silver rods each leading into deeper regions of the machine. Those rods may be likened to fuses that connect one part of the machine with another. You will notice that the machine is divided into five parts, connected by four fuses. The first part of the machine is already in action, and has been for many years. It is in the midst of sorting out the minor probabilities of material creation. Occasionally, as it reaches a solution point, it emanates a new probability wave, which accounts for the vanishing acts we have experienced.

"Very shortly now it will pass to a more advanced state of mathematics, when it has exhausted the mathematical possibilities of the particular stage upon which is it working. This second stage will greatly increase the frequency and area of its working.… The third, fourth, and fifth stages are so profoundly deep in mathematics and electronic probability that it would be futile to try to explain them. But this we know: the fifth stage means the complete dissolution of every material thing. The only thing that can stop it is the removal of the fuses which interconnect the sections."

"Will it be difficult?" Mexone asked, looking into the machine.

The Amazon and Abna exchanged looks. Viona saw the action and gave a grim smile.

"Well, let's have it! It won't be easy, I take it?"

"Without exaggeration, it will be the most dangerous job we've ever tackled," Abna said frankly. "That is, if our calculations are right, and there is no reason why they shouldn't be. Each fuse must be removed with infinite care. If this is not done, the two parts of the machine connected by that fuse will short-circuit, with disastrous results. Maybe even a gigantic explosion. When the fuse has been taken out, a safety fuse will have to be inserted in its place while the required section of the machine is rendered dead—which means disconnecting all power wires leading to it. The safety fuse will be a temporary affair capable of carrying the power load for a definite time only. We'll have to make those ourselves. From the taking out of the fuse to fitting the temporary one we have about thirty minutes. If it is not put in by then, heaven knows what will happen, since part of the machine will be functioning independently of the other part. Each fuse leads to a definite area of the machine, the last areas being the most tricky and complicated. I will take on the last fuse, and you, Mexone, the second. Is that perfectly clear?"

"Perfectly," Viona and Mexone nodded together.

"There must be no tremoring. No quivering, but slow and painstaking care," Abna warned. "You're dealing with a mathematical high explosive, and one slip can destroy the planet, and even maybe the universe."

"From what," the Amazon asked, "do we make the temporary fuses? Go back to the *Ultra*?"

"No, that will take too long. We may have precious little time as it is." Abna looked at the fuses for a moment and then nodded to himself.

"We've got the material all around us—silver. A first-class conductor of electric current. Better dig some out of the cavern walls."

He did not waste any further time talking, but set off up the crater side. The Amazon, Viona, and Mexone followed him, then proceeded to follow his example in digging out chunks of pure silver from amidst the rock. To mould the silver into the required size was not a difficult job with the heat-guns they had at their disposal, so within halt an hour their rough fuses had been made.

"Good enough," Abna said, leading the way back. "Now we can start—and may good luck be with us."

"All we need is interruption by one of the monsters at the vital stage," Mexone remarked grimly. "Any of you thought of that possibility? Because the brutes seem to be quiet at the moment doesn't mean we're going to be left in peace."

Abna shrugged. "Have to take our chance on that." He looked at his daughter. "Ready, Viona?"

She braced herself, half stooping toward the innards of the machine.

With infinite care Viona went to work. Abna, the Amazon, and Mexone remained rigid close beside her, watching every move and alert for the first sign of trouble. But Viona knew exactly what she was doing, and her hands were slender and rock steady. Very carefully she unfastened the curious-looking clamp at one of the fuses and pulled gently. Immediately the fuse came free, but the clamp snapped shut with the tightness of a vice. She paused for a moment and gave Abna a questioning glance.

"Carry on," he said quietly. "I expected that. That was why I said temporary fuses, so they can be slipped roughly into place. Once these genuine fuses are taken out it will take too long to replace them."

"When I've got the fuse right out, you're going to start dismantling this first section—or at least render it harmless?" Viona questioned.

"That's it. Keep going."

Viona went to work again, pulling and twisting gently, her hands buried in, just clear of, a maze of power wires which fed the heart of the first section of the machine. She hazarded a guess that to touch any of the exposed terminals would probably be the end of her, but she still persisted. Then she breathed a little more freely as the final end of the fuse dislodged itself from its socket. There was a sharp snap as the socket closed immovably and Viona lifted the fuse free.

"Whew!" she whistled, and felt a trickle of perspiration creep down her face.

Abna smiled and clapped her on the shoulder, then as he was about to speak he stopped again at the sound of another voice.

"So my friends, you escaped after all!"

Still holding the dislodged fuse in her hand, Viona turned in amazement. So did the Amazon, Abna, and Mexone—to stare in consternation at Scind and a gathering of his followers only a few feet away. They had arrived in silence, and in the intensity of their concentration the four had never noticed.

"As well I came when I did," Scind continued, coming forward with a queer-shaped gun in his hand. "I suspected something might have happened when I noticed—or at least it was reported to me—that a hole had been torn in the surface of our world not far from our dwellings. The kind of hole that is sometimes made by a transportation to Paradise. I decided to come and see what was transpiring. So you've decided to wreck the machine?"

"Yes, because necessity demands it. Unless something is done quickly, the whole machine will blow up and perhaps destroy the planet. Here is one of the main parts which has just been removed."

Viona held up the fuse and instantly Scind snatched it from her. His eyes moved to Abna.

"I imagine this is your planning, my friend—still interfering in matters that don't concern you! Put this fuse back!"

"Too dangerous," Abna replied. "The only solution

is a temporary fuse—and that has to be put in quickly."

Unwittingly his gaze strayed to the silver makeshifts on the floor. Scind saw the rods of silver immediately, and his face hardened slightly.

"So you planned a deliberate wrecking of this machine? You speak of temporary fuses—these things down here, I suppose. If they are not put in, what will happen?"

"I've already told you. The destruction of the entire universe."

Scind reflected for a moment, deeply. The Amazon clenched her fists slowly and cast a look at the many guns trained on her. As yet the situation was anything but in her favor.

"It would seem," Scind observed at last, "that in attempting to dismantle this machine, you have provided all of us with a shortcut to Paradise. For that much I can thank you."

Abna stared in amazement. This was an aspect that had never occurred to him, and if it did nothing else, it at least showed how completely Scind was sold on the idea that annihilation meant eternal bliss.

"You said that there is only a certain time in which to put in a temporary fuse?" Scind asked. "If that is not done, the machine will create disaster.... That is good hearing. There need no longer be a long wait before all of us can reach Paradise—you included, my friends."

With that he picked up the temporary fuses from the floor, together with the one he had snatched from Viona.

"Since Paradise is so near, we will let things take their course," he said. "I will dispose of these objects and then we will see what happens."

With that he began to retreat, gun in one hand and fuses in the other. By degrees he worked himself up the side of the crater, then finally turned and headed into its deeper depths.

"Now what?" Mexone demanded, horrified. "There isn't time to make more fuses, even if this gang permitted us."

Abna swung to the gathered people, still leveling guns.

"Which among you speaks my language?" he demanded. "Half a dozen were given that gift—including Doxa and Scind. Surely there are some among you who can—"

"I can," said a woman, raising her hand.

"And I," said one of the men in the forefront, holding a gun.

"Then listen to me," Abna said urgently. "Unless I do certain things to this machine quickly every one of us is going to be killed—horribly. There will be no swift transportation to perfect bliss as Scind seems to think. You heard what he said?"

"We heard," acknowledged the man in the forefront. "Since he spoke in your language, only those of us who know it understood what he said. And I think he's mad."

"Then tell the rest of your people that quickly!" Abna ordered.

The little man nodded and talked quickly with the others for a while, then he turned back.

"They believe, too, that Scind is mad. Whether he is or not, we have no love for him because of his cruelty since he became our leader. We do not want to die horribly. We have enough faith in your science to believe that you are trying to help. We are willing to aid you and turn against Scind when he returns."

"Where do you think he's gone?" demanded the Amazon.

"Probably to the regions of molten metal farther down in the bowels of the planet, there to rid himself of those important fuses you mentioned—" The little man threw away his gun. "There! That is how much we are prepared to help."

"Right!" Abna cast an urgent look at the machine. "We have got to have silver out of the cavern wall quickly, to make a fuse. There isn't a moment to lose. I'll show you what to do. Vi, you can—"

Abna paused in surprise. Though Viona and Mexone had come quickly to his side, there was no sign of the Amazon. Silently and mysteriously she had disappeared.

CHAPTER SIX
THE END OF SCIND

Once she had realized that the little people were no longer in favor of Scind, the Amazon had moved swiftly, her own private longing for revenge occupying the main place in her thoughts. Now, her headlight in full blast, she was speeding down the passages and trails of the underworld, going deeper with every moment, in the hope that her pursuit would lead her to Scind.

Once or twice as she sped silently down the crudely carved galleries the Amazon fancied she heard the stirring of giant beasts, but she did not stay long enough to make sure. She had only one aim—Scind. And at last she saw him ahead down a long tunnel as she turned a corner. Quickly she switched off her lamp, wondering how he was able to find his way in the dark.

Then it was she realized that at these depths everything was lighted with a satanic red glow. The source of it came from somewhere ahead—some kind of enormous volcanic crater, which at the moment was fortunately quiescent. Against this red glare—the rocks and spurs standing out sharply in total blackness—Scind was silhouetted as he moved swiftly. But not for long. Reaching what seemed to be a precipice, he came to a halt and stood considering.

He did not think for long. The Amazon sprang suddenly and Scind had just time to see her hurtling down upon him. He brought up his gun to firing level but it went spinning out of his hand and into the crater as the Amazon closed with him

Mightily though he struggled, he did not stand much chance against her iron strength. Almost instantly he was knocked over on to his back, his hand releasing the makeshift fuses, together with the genuine one. They rolled to the edge of the ledge and there were stopped by the unevenness of the rockery.

"Since you won't learn by plain talking there has to be another way," the Amazon panted. "Believe me, Scind, it was not my intention to do this, but—"

Scind heaved, desperation lending him unexpected strength. Unprepared for it, the Amazon pitched sideways and only just succeeded in grasping an imbedded piece of rock. Otherwise she would certainly have rolled off the ledge into the crater,

Just in time she saw Scind charging at her in a final maddened rush. She had no time to defend herself, so she lay prone—and that proved Scind's undoing.

Meeting no expected resistance, his bull rush carried him beyond the Amazon, unable to stop himself. He went clean over the rock ledge and with a ghastly howl sailed outwards into the fumes and steam. He dropped head over heels—and was gone.

Slowly, her face set, the Amazon got to her feet. She looked into the crater, shrugged to herself, then picked up the four experimental fuses and went back like the wind through the galleries and tunnels. Finally arriving back at the machine, she elbowed her way through the men and women.

"Forty seconds left—" Abna was saying. "We'll never—"

"Forty seconds?" the Amazon exclaimed. "Right—get busy!"

"Vi!" Abna cried, as she hurried toward him with the fuses extended in her hand. "Where have you been—?"

"Never mind that. Here—take the right fuse. I'll explain afterwards."

Working at desperate speed, Abna selected the correct one, threw out the makeshift one which had been made in the interval, and quickly wired the slender silver rod into position. Then he slowly relaxed and breathed hard.

"That," he muttered, "was a close one! Far too lose for comfort...."

"What went wrong?" the Amazon asked, putting down the remaining three fuses on the rockery. "Didn't the rush one fit?"

"No. It was hastily done—Mexone and Viona improvised it and the people here helped. It wasn't a good job. I had to do some dismantling of section one while they worked. Thank heaven you turned up when you did and straightened things out.... I suppose you chased Scind? You must have done to get the fuses."

"Scind will no longer be a problem," The Amazon gave a grim smile and turned to the people. "You understand that?" she asked, and the four remaining who understood English promptly nodded.

"Good," Abna smiled. "Well, our next job is to carry on with the dismantling of this machine. Or better still, maybe we had better have a meal and a rest before we start again. See what you can do, Viona, will you?"

Viona nodded and set about the task of preparing a meal from the provisions they had with them—packed and on their backs in tabloid form at the time Scind had invaded the *Ultra*. In less than fifteen minutes the four were seated on the crater floor, the scene illumined by their detached headlamps, with the little men and women watching them in silent interest.

The Amazon took time out to bathe her cut face and then, refreshed, she turned and looked at the others.

"Who's the next operative? Mexone?"

"Right." Mexone got to his feet with a set face. "I think you said things get more difficult as they go on, Abna?"

"That's inevitable, because we're going deeper into the involved mathematical set-up of the machine, beside which an electronic computer would be a mere nothing."

The Amazon and Mexone moved over to the machine, and Abna and Viona followed behind. Mexone looked into the complicated depths, at the first and second stages linked by the rough fuse, and then he prepared for action. Gently he lowered his hands into the wilderness of the second stage.

He began to pull on the fuse bar carefully. It twisted in his hands and became free, the clamp instantly shutting down immovably as had the previous one.

"Okay," he muttered, relaxing for a moment. "The current is disconnected. You can start dismantling the second stage, Abna."

Abna did not need the hint: he went to work right away. For a while Mexone watched him, then recovering his strength and nerve, he set about unscrewing the second clamp.

"Ten minutes left," the Amazon said. "Better get busy with the dismantling. Now what's your trouble, Mexone?"

"I haven't got the steadiness or the grip. See what you can do."

The Amazon took the screwdriver from him while Viona stood by with the temporary fuse. After missing the first time, the Amazon secured the driver in the screw slot the second time and then paused for a moment.

"Never go straight on exerting yourself," she advised. "When you've reached the objective, pause for a moment, then throw everything you've got into the effort—like this!"

Abruptly the muscles of her arm bulged under the black, tight-sleeved costume she was wearing. Mexone watched in silent amazement as the screw slowly turned under irresistible pressure and at last loosened itself.

Promptly, working at top speed, the Amazon pulled the screw out, then swiftly unfastened the smaller ones. Meantime Abna was busy disconnecting every second-stage terminal he could see.

"Three minutes left," Viona announced anxiously, glancing at her watch.

The Amazon nodded tautly, and tugged out the last screw. Then she carefully eased out the fuse end and pulled it free. Viona took it from her.

"Ready, Abna?" the Amazon questioned sharply, and pulling free a final coil of wire, he nodded.

"Ready."

In a matter of moments the Amazon had fixed the temporary fuse across the terminals. Nothing apparently happened as the clamps were bridged, but paper calculations had shown that the build-up of current in the still functioning stages of the machine now had a chance to spend itself into the various storage batteries and power potentials of the disabled areas.

"Screw clamps again," the Amazon sighed after surveying. "I can only assume the idea is to make it too difficult for anybody to remove them."

She took Mexone's screwdriver, which she still had in her hand, and turned to tackle the first clamp. The smaller screws were comparatively easy and finally the end of the fuse was ready for moving.

"Right!" she said, grasping it and glancing at Abna. "You can start dismantling any moment—"

She pulled the fuse end clear and at that instant something happened. The moment the fuse no longer bridged the gap, the machine reacted—and in a most devastating way. From its depths there sprang up a pale orange glow. Where it was coming from was not altogether clear. Perhaps it was some overflow of power. The Amazon waited for a second and tried to jam the fuse quickly back, but this was impossible since the clamp had shut itself, and there was no firm link in which to fix the fuse end.

As the orange glow increased, peculiarly hurtful to the eye, she sprang back. It was just as well she did so, for in a matter of seconds the glow had changed to blue-white of ever-increasing intensity.

"We've done something, but I don't know what," the Amazon panted, her back to the drenching light as she glanced at Abna. "And we've got to do something with the fuse half out."

"Probably some upset in the spectrum scale," Abna responded. "When you shifted the fuse you perhaps somehow rendered the spectrum probabilities unstable. What about your goggles? You all have them on."

The Amazon felt at her throat. The goggles, which had originally been intended to combat the brilliance of the surface, were hanging around her neck. Quickly she slipped them in position and then ventured to look toward the machine. She gave a nod of satisfaction.

"Still pretty bright, but I'll risk it."

Abna came up silently, goggles in place, ready for immediate action when the fuse was right out. So, peering into the glare, the Amazon began to work on the other end of the fuse, shifting the screw, and then beginning the usual process of extraction. At least illumination was not her problem, and she worked fast but carefully. With a sigh of relief she finally pulled the fuse free.

Abna promptly went to work, unscrewing terminals and uncoiling wires as fast as he could go. During this process the light suddenly expired and intense darkness—or so it seemed—shut down. Immediately the Amazon pulled off her goggles and switched on her headlamp. The light from it seemed dirty yellow by comparison with the actinic brilliance that they had been experiencing.

"Eyes all right?" Abna asked sharply, and the Amazon nodded.

"Aching a good deal, but still functioning."

"I don't think it was anything more than ordinary light—concentrated. Must have been spectrum shift—"

The Amazon fitted the temporary fuse, ready to fit it into place when Abna had finished dismantling the third stage.

"How are you making out, Abna?" she inquired.

"Practically finished." His powerful hands were still busy with the terminals. "Just these two to do—There!"

Promptly as he withdrew his hands, the Amazon slipped the temporary fuse into place. She half expected something would happen from the machine, but all was well. Taking a deep breath of relief, she looked again at the little people. They were wreathed in smiles until she ordered them to leave now because of the danger. They left obediently.

Abna detached his micro-camera from his equipment. Without further explanation, he went to work to photograph the weird machine once again from every possible angle. With puzzled frowns the others watched him.

The Amazon said: "I've asked you before, and I'm asking you again: why do you need to photograph this thing?"

"It would take too long to explain now. Tell you later." Abna slipped the camera back on his belt and then prepared for action. "Right! Now for the last fuse."

CHAPTER SEVEN
MONSTER ATTACK

The fuse linking the fourth and fifth stages of the electronic monster was definitely a tough one. Instead of the usual screw clamps, it had massive jaws of silver, pulled taut by an immensely powerful spring. It might as well have been part of the planet itself for all the impression Abna made in pulling on it.

"Seems to me," Abna said, desisting in his efforts for a moment, "as though these scientists deliberately made things tougher as they went on. I'll have to pry the spring apart, and keep your fingers crossed for what may happen when I disconnect the final stages."

He pulled an instrument not unlike a tire lever from his belt and proceeded to wedge the end between the tight coils of the spring. Thus, by exerting all his strength, he managed slowly to force the spring upwards to the limit of its extent.

"Quickly!" he instructed the Amazon. "Pull the fuse out!"

She did so, but at this stage only one came free. Abna released the spring and it flew back into place with a powerful twanging note.

"Now for the other end," Abna said, and maneuvered his 'tire lever' downwards. He was just on the point of repeating the same process as on the previous occasion when a dull growling noise made him glance up. The Amazon, Viona, and Mexone glanced up at the same moment and caught their breath in alarm.

Standing at the top of the crater, its upper lip twitching in hate, was an animal of the cat species. But what a cat! No saber-toothed tiger of earthly birth had ever approached the dimensions of this one. It stood as high as an elephant, and like the rest of these underground denizens, its eyes were enormous. In this case jade green and unblinking, staring in the headlamps with hypnotic intensity.

"This looks like trouble," Abna muttered, feeling for his gun. "If only it had come before I got the fuse out! We've got about twenty-eight minutes to dispose of the brute before we put in a temporary fuse—"

"Give me an ordinary tiger and I'd tear it in pieces with my bare hands," the Amazon muttered, "but this one is a different proposition. I'll do my best. You carry on."

Abna hesitated, then he reached to the last fuse on the floor to put it in a place of safety. His movements seemed to interest the giant tiger for its eyes followed him intensely. Again the red jaws opened to emit a growl—then the creature started moving down the crater side, its enormous padded feet exhibiting claws as large as grapple-hooks as it moved.

"Get behind!" the Amazon snapped, as Viona and

Mexone pulled their guns. "I'll deal with this beauty...."

She went down on one knee to get better aim, then as the monster came bounding into the sights of her proton gun she released the stream of searing energy.

The howl of anguish the beast gave made the floor shake. It stopped in mid-movement, a gigantic blur of striped fur, and reared upwards. The beam had seared it painfully, but it had by no means put it out of action.

Tense-faced, the Amazon waited, knowing that the only chance was the gun. To use a bomb at such close quarters would be disastrous. Abna gave one look and then went on forcing the second spring of the fuse.

Abruptly, as the beast paused for a moment to inspect its injuries, the Amazon glanced towards Abna.

"Abna...." Her voice was a hoarse, strained whisper.

"What?" He was in the midst of prising the fuse spring, Viona holding the fuse and waiting to pull it free.

"I think the noise the little people made in getting away from here must have attracted this brute. Hope there are no more like it!"

Abna muttered something inaudible, then he said aloud: "Quick—the fuse! Pull it out, Viona."

Viona did as she was told, but before she could put in the temporary fuse the tiger got on the move again. It came hurtling down the crater side, obviously having made up its mind that these four intruders had no right in its domain. The Amazon held her gun steady, never flinching, and pressed the button as the brute came into the sights. To her horror, nothing happened! The charges had exhausted themselves.

With split seconds in hand she hurled herself to one side, missing by a fraction one of the brute's outflung paws, then desperately reloaded the weapon from her belt. The terrible claws were half as long as a tall man and could easily have ripped a human being open from head to foot. With a crash the brute hit the machine, but already Abna and Viona had fled for safety. Snarling, licking its chops, the giant animal looked from one side to the other.

Abna, Viona, and Mexone all had their guns at the ready by now as, together, they maneuvered to the far side of the crater. The tiger watched them, then with its usual lightning speed the tiger sprang. It ran straight into a crossfire of four proton guns. If it had howled with pain before, it was as nothing compared to its present convulsions. Stopping in mid-leap before the onslaught, it crashed to the floor and lashed and writhed with stupendous force, the lower part of its body almost reduced to ashes.

The air stank of burning fur and flesh as, keeping her position, the Amazon fired charge after charge into the brute, bringing it each time to a fresh madness.

"I think that's about it," the Amazon said at last, turning a strained face. "And all the time I'm wondering how many more brutes there are like this around."

Nobody said anything further, but the Amazon at least was thinking how lucky she had been to avoid such monsters in her excursion to the lower reaches.… Then Abna moved forward.

He studied the mutilated, dead tiger. The moments were fast slipping in which to put in the spare machine fuse and dismantle the final stages.

"Time I got a move on," he said. "I've been interrupted enough."

He picked up the temporary fuse and fastened it securely to one clamp, but before he could complete the job there came yet another interruption. A creature of indescribable form, evidently attracted by the noise, had emerged from the depths to investigate. At the moment it was at the top of the crater with only its head and shoulders visible. More of it came into view as it advanced, and it seemed as though its colossal body would never end.

"Look at the thing!" the Amazon breathed incredulously to Viona and Mexone. "Did you ever see anything to equal it?"

They shook their heads dumbly. The creature resembled an ape in general formation, but when its whole body came into sight it must have stood at least thirty feet tall—a solid packed mass of iron muscles, its long arms touching the floor and its hideous narrow-browed face terminating in a wide, snarling mouth.

It took only seconds to absorb these details, then the giant ape was streaking down the side of the crater, its little, red-rimmed eyes filled with homicidal viciousness.

"Look out, Abna!" the Amazon yelled, training her gun again, and Abna looked up from his task.

Before he could finish his fuse job he leaped to one

side, just in time to dodge the sweeping onrush of the creature. Even as it was the vast body brushed against him and knocked him flying.

Instantly he was up, as the ape twirled around. Snatching out his proton gun he fired it hastily, delivering a burning swathe across the brute's chest that stopped it for a moment. The moment was enough for Abna to race across to the others—then in a tight little quartet with their guns drawn they stood waiting for what was to happen next.

"We've got to finish this job quickly," Abna exclaimed. "I haven't fixed that fuse yet and time's running out."

From sheer desperation he fired again—and again, the last fiery barb striking straight to the beast's heart. It lurched wildly and then fell heavily with arms extended, the bulk of its body across the machine. There it remained—motionless.

"I think we've settled it," the Amazon said, as there was no further movement. "Better see."

Using every caution, her gun tilted in readiness, she went slowly forward. In a moment or two she realized that the brute was quite dead. The final blow to the heart had finished it. But the difficulty now lay in the fact that the monster had entirely covered the machine in its fall.

"Got to shift it somehow," Abna said, with a glance at his watch. "I've only got five minutes to fix that fuse. Come on, all of you."

He seized hold of the immense, hairy bulk and

pushed. It was like trying to lift a century-old oak tree out of the ground. The ape was dead weight and of enormous heaviness. Fiercely though the four sweated and heaved, they accomplished precisely nothing.

"How about blasting away its body to allow you room to get into the machine?" the Amazon demanded. "We might—"

"Too late now," Abna said grimly. "Time's up."

They stood looking at each other, full of the awareness that, according to their calculations on paper, something ought to happen. The entire power of the strange machine was now being concentrated into two stages, and when power had no outlet—

"First time we've failed in our mission," Abna said. "We don't know what will happen now so we'd better get away from here while we're in one piece. Get out to the surface if we can through that tunnel they blocked up."

He turned and led the way purposefully up the crater side. The others had just joined him at the summit when a sudden sound made them glance back. It was a noise somehow reminiscent of a squirting soda-siphon.

"That sounds like power arcing across somewhere," Abna commented. "The trouble we expected is going to happen, I'm afraid—"

He had hardly spoken before the weird electronic machine exploded. Strangely enough, it did so without a sound, but it certainly generated tremendous shockwaves. The four were abruptly flung from their feet by a violent earth tremor, while at the same time the machine exploded outwards in a thousand pieces of silver fragments, wires, flashes of light, and bewildering displays of colors. The body of the ape disintegrated at the same time.

Even with the actual explosion of the machine the shockwaves did not cease. They billowed along the ground and the quartet hung on desperately to the rockery as though it were a boat in a rough sea.

A shock—or series of shocks—of this nature in the deep underground could only have one result. The very rocks themselves started to dislodge, raining down in ever-increasing thunder, battering the quartet as they lay flat and tried to protect themselves.

Then gradually the disturbance subsided. All was quiet save for that still-continuing sound like a squirting soda-siphon.

Slowly, very slowly, Abna began to raise himself and shook the rubbish from him. He could feel blood trickling from a dozen cuts and bruises. Gray with dust, the Amazon, Viona, and Mexone rose, too, their well-protected headlamps still blazing through the hazy atmosphere.

"All in one piece?" Abna inquired.

"Plenty of gashes and scratches but no actual bones broken," the Amazon said, after a quick checkup. "Nothing we won't all of us soon get over— What's that fizzing noise?" she demanded abruptly.

"I'm just about to find out."

Abna stood up and moved forward, moving to what had formerly been the crater top. Now its outline was changed enormously. Puzzled, he stood staring into the crater where the machine had been. Something was there, like a small core of violet light. It generated a curious tingling sensation even at this distance. Suddenly he realized what it was and dropped his dark goggles over his eyes.

"What is it?" the Amazon asked, coming to his side and looking. "Something still burning down there?"

"Yes—and it isn't just the escape of power from the wires either. It's a legacy of the machine's inside. Unless I'm mistaken, that's a core of consuming energy, and its emitting a good deal of ultraviolet. Better pull your goggles down to protect your eyes."

The Amazon did so. So did Viona and Mexone as they came up. In silence they stood viewing the sputtering, slowly enlarging spot of ultraviolet in the depths of the crater.

"This," Abna said at length, "is worse than I expected. Have you noticed something about that core of energy? It's growing larger all the time and it is in the form of a circle. It leaves behind it a total black. Let's risk going closer."

He led the way down the crater side, and with every step forward that was taken the emanation of the sizzling energy became more noticeable, until at really close quarters it was akin to intense sun-burning.

"We can't stay long: it's dangerous." Abna came to a stop and pointed. "See what I mean? This energy is now in a slowly expanding circle. It leaves behind it a depthless nothing, which shows it is going downwards as well as outward."

The Amazon said slowly: "You mean that, like a flowing tide, this released energy from the machine is slowly turning all things material into—nothing?"

"Yes. The 'nothing' only appears as that to our eyes. Actually the 'nothing' is some new state which we cannot perceive. Following the law of chain-reaction, the whole planet will finally be eaten into annihilation."

For some reason Mexone found a bright spot in this cheerless announcement.

"Then in a roundabout way we've accomplished our purpose? We set out to destroy this machine, and we've done it—even though it involves the destruction of the whole planet in the process. Once the planet is gone there won't be any more danger, Abna, will there?"

"I hardly think so. The process will not continue into space because there won't be anything material to 'bite' on, so to speak. It worries me, though, that it means death for the child-people."

"Yes, it does," the Amazon muttered. "In accomplishing our end we've also lamentably failed. We've protected the universe at the cost of a planet and its people. What's the answer, Abna? We surely can't leave the child-people to their fate?"

Abna shrugged, though he was thoughtful. He led the way to the wall where the tunnel had been blocked. Added to that there were now hundreds of tons of rock and boulders in addition, shaken down from the roof.

"Could we try some of our bombs?" Viona suggested,

but after a survey Abna shook his head.

"Wouldn't do, Viona. Too dangerous in such a confined space. Look at those rock pinnacles up there! Any more violent disturbance and down they'll come, too. Better try manual effort."

So they promptly set to work heaving and tugging the mighty stones to one side, but after half an hour of this it became more than obvious that they were doomed to failure. There were so many of the rocks, and some of them were of such enormous size it would take days and nights of time before they got a clearance. And added to this was the constant danger of dislodging some of the higher pinnacles, which would immediately precipitate an avalanche.

"No use," Abna declared at length. "We'll never get out this way. We'd better return to the chasm by which we gained ingress and see if our friends remembered to leave the ropes hanging. I expect they did, but habit may have dictated otherwise. Never tell with child minds."

The idea certainly had possibilities, so they began to move quickly, retracing their way as well as they could remember it and leaving behind that hissing, expanding area of energy that was spelling the doom of a planet.

So they resumed the advance, plodding down passages, across big stretches of cavern, always clinging to the route that provided them with familiar landmarks. Then suddenly they were stopped! A veritable mountain of rock barred the way invincibly, evidently brought down in the recent shocks.

"It may be miles thick," Abna said, studying it. "No getting away from it: there's no way out that way."

"We're getting nowhere pretty fast," the Amazon said grimly, sitting down on a rock spur. "What do we do, Abna?"

He shrugged. "Afraid I'm no wiser than you, Vi."

"That's where you're wrong, even though I hate to admit it. You've got us out of spots as tough as this before—by mind force. Why can't you do it now?"

"You mean transfer us through the rock by mental compulsion? On this planet the conditions are different to any we've yet experienced. I can sense it when I try to concentrate. The shifting of electronic probabilities is a very real thing. They exist in the air, even though the machine producing them has ceased to function as such. It has, however, produced just enough confusion to upset my concentrations. I can no longer be sure of the defiance of materiality because even the materiality is in a state of uncertainty."

CHAPTER EIGHT
THE RESURRECTED WORLD

The Amazon roused herself from silence. She looked at the faces of the others, and finally at Abna.

"Then our last chance has gone?"

"I refuse to believe that, Vi; it sounds to much like defeatism. We have just got to get out or else perish—and that pretty quickly. I can think of only one way, and that is to take the risk of bombing our way out."

The Amazon gave a dubious glance. "Suppose we start an avalanche?"

"Better to take that chance than stick here and rot—and we can he pretty certain the rest of the tunnels will finish up like this one, in a blank wall."

The Amazon did not argue any further, realizing the inevitability of the situation. With Mexone and Viona she moved to the farther distances of the cavern and finally settled down behind a high screen of protective rock. Abna stayed long enough to take a small-type bomb from his supplies and set the time-fuse, then he hurried across and joined the others.

The quartet crouched behind the rock shelter had one vision of a blinding flash, then their ears were deafened by the explosion itself. Rocks and small stones rained down upon them, together with clouds of dust, but apart from minor cuts they were unhurt as at last the disturbance subsided. They waited anxiously for the growling rumble of dislodged higher rockery, but it did not come.

"So far, so good," Abna commented. "Better see what's happened."

He hurried from the protection of the rock to closely survey the wall, which had taken the full shock of the blast. Almost immediately he glimpsed a pock-marked interlacing of light high in the rocks.

"We're through!" he cried in delight. "Or at least we soon shall be. Take a look."

The vision above was enough to satisfy. Proton guns were yanked out and there began the task of blasting away what remained of rock, until finally there was an opening easily big enough to admit of their passage. Then they began the slow and difficult climb up the shaft's rugged walls.

The first to emerge was Abna, narrowing his eyes in the glare of the newly risen sun. The Amazon, Viona and Mexone followed shortly afterwards and, conscious of an enormous relief, they stood looking about them.

"Not so very far away from our objective," Abna commented, nodding to the not-far-distant settlement with its single spire of silver reaching skywards and—in the distance beyond—the enormous bulk of the *Ultra*. "We'd better get moving and tell these folks what's going on."

They began moving, and they had not proceeded very far before the child-people came hurrying toward them. Abna raised his hand for them to pause, then when they were congregated in full numbers he began speaking.

"I regret to have to tell you, my friends, that something has gone wrong—not anything of our own doing, but because a monster interfered with our plans.... Interpret that for them, someone, will you?" He paused whilst this was done.

"There is no sense in trying to hide anything from you," Abna continued, "for it will become self-evident soon enough. I don't expect you to understand the technical details, but your world is bound in a very short time to crumble into pieces. An atomic chain reaction has been started which all our science cannot stop. Or if it could, it would not be in time."

The people became anxiously silent as the interpreter spoke this next bit. He himself waited with a worried frown as Abna thought for a moment, then asked a question:

"It is somewhat late in the day to ask if you people are the only ones on this planet, but I want to know."

"We are the only ones who approach a civilized order," the interpreter responded. "We have gathered together as one tribe from all parts of the planet. We're the survivors of the scientists, as I suppose Doxa told you. What others there are can only be few, and they'll be more or less homeless wanderers."

Abna nodded slowly. "Which means you're all more or less congregated together. And there'll be—maybe 500 of you all told?"

"About," he conceded. "Why?"

"I think I have a plan—a plan whereby you can not only escape to safety, but start again in a fresh green world—a little paradise of its own."

The Amazon, Viona, and Mexone looked at one another then towards Abna. He smiled slightly.

"Does it sound crazy?" he grinned.

"More than that," the Amazon told him. "It is!"

"Not with the neighbor-world of Antara at some fifty million miles distance."

The Amazon started. "I'd forgotten that. But it's a dead world! A burned-out planet! Certainly no paradise."

"It can be," Abna said grimly. We have instruments aboard the *Ultra* capable of molding that huge cosmic cinder into a new world—a world that is safe from the atomic disintegration that is even now eating the heart out of this one. But we'll have to act fast."

The Amazon's violet eyes gleamed as her scientific imagination embraced with the idea. She snapped her fingers.

"Of course we can do it! Air, water, trees for the absorption of toxics—"

"Exactly," Abna assented. "And the sooner the better...." He turned back to the interpreter.

"We are going to leave you, my friend," he said quietly. "At all possible speed we are traveling to your neighbor world of Antara, there to create a new paradise for you. Have faith that we shall return."

"Unto the end," the little man said fervently. "If you do not, then it would seem our doom is certain." He brightened a little. "But I at least have faith that you will come back."

Abna nodded and turned swiftly. "Come. We've got to hurry."

* * * * * * *

At the *Ultra*'s mounting speed of many millions of miles an hour, it wasn't long before the hulk of Antara was within easy viewing distance, but in the intervening time the quartet had slept and ate, to awaken now thoroughly refreshed for the task in hand.

As the cinder of a world drew nearer Abna turned to the switchboard and cut down the power. Even so, Antara appeared to rush silently through the infinite, growing ever larger and revealing its starkly naked outline. Blackened rock was the only thing visible, from which every other formation had been eradicated. At least it gave some idea of the frightful convulsion that had seized it at some time in the past.

Finally Abna brought the *Ultra* to a comparative crawl and swept it down through the airless heights to a monstrous plain, which looked exactly like pumice stone. With a slight jar the machine came to rest and the hum of the power plant ceased. In silence the quartet stood looking out of the window.

Nowhere a sign of life, a shrub, even a blade of

grass. Here indeed was a world dead in every sense of the word.

"Well," Abna said presently, "it's time we got to work. We're not here to explore, but to act. Before we leave this planet, it has got to have all the qualities of a Garden of Eden.... All right, Vi, get busy with the pumping apparatus. I'll check the mixture."

The Amazon nodded and turned to the apparatus for the mixing of gases. In any case, there were three already practically full of oxygen, hydrogen, and nitrogen, for their own consumption aboard the *Ultra*—and more could readily be manufactured in the atomic 'breakdown' chamber, a neighbor tank used for the changing of gas ingredients, or pressure.

"All set to project outside?" Abna asked, beside the switch panel.

"All set." The Amazon held her yellow hand over the controls for the outflow of gas.

"Let it go!" Abna ordered, and simultaneously switched on the power, which projected the gas to the exterior by means of special nozzles.

By the time the sun was setting the job was done, and there was something rather wonderful in seeing the dense starlit black of the sky change to pale blue as the sunlight was refracted. There were even clouds forming as the heat of the sun changed the density of the atmospheric layers.

"Lastly, the seeds," Abna said, and looked to where Viona had sorted out a selection of various types—all of them the seeds of other worlds, since the original

Ultra, containing many Earth specimens, had been destroyed in their travels. The seeds they had collected from other worlds had been stored, and studied and cataloged during leisure moments, and the information retained in the *Ultra*'s data banks. It had been a simple task for Viona to program the central computer to select self-propagating plants that did not require pollination by insects. Antara was presently devoid of all native life forms, and that included insects.

"At least they'll become living plants," the Amazon said, "and that's all we need to rid the air of toxics, and to provide food crops for the Tucans."

Abna nodded. "While I control the *Ultra*, you, Viona, and Mexone, can feed these plant seeds to the 'cultivated' areas through the floor traps. It won't take us long to circumnavigate the planet."

So it was arranged, and in the rising glare of the day the *Ultra* flew with steady speed over the rejuvenated planet, across lakes that had been created in the darkness, over rocky mountain ranges, and across lonely, desolate plains. Over the pulverized areas the seeds were dropped—and again in the night regions as the *Ultra* flew to the dark side of the planet.

Until at last it came back to the starting point and Abna set it down on the rocky plain.

"Well, does that finish it?" the Amazon asked, glancing outside to the blue sky with its drifting clouds.

"Almost," Abna reflected for a moment. "We'll go around the planet once more and turn energizing beams onto the seed areas. That should stimulate the seeds to enormous, speed-up activity, and by the time we're back with the first batch of child-people the seeds will have sprouted halfway to maturity. I'll guide the ship as before. You three others operate the beams."

They nodded and moved to their various positions. Once again Abna set the *Ultra* in motion and, moving more slowly this time, the planet was circuited yet again, at a rate compatible with the time needed for projecting the beams on to the seeded areas beneath.... So at length, when the *Ultra* came to a halt again on the same plain, Abna gave a grin of satisfaction.

"The best few hours' work we have ever done," he commented. "Old worlds restored while you wait." Then, catching the Amazon's cool look of disapproval, he turned back again to the switch panel. "Time to collect the first of the child-people, and let's hope the disintegration hasn't spread too far."

He set the power levers in position again and the *Ultra* swept upwards to the blue sky with its usual perfect ease. The four stood gazing down for a moment at the receding world which they had so miraculously changed, then as it grew remote and the void once again took over they drifted from the window and prepared once again for a well-earned meal and a rest.

* * * * * * *

Their return to the world of Tuca was hailed with obvious delight by the child-people. It seemed as though nearly every one of them turned out to give a greeting as the *Ultra* settled down in its former position about a mile from the settlement.

"We're going to have to make a lot of journeys," the Amazon said. "There are 500 of them, and that's a good deal. How many do you think we can manage at a time?"

"About 100, stowing them away in every part of the vessel," Abna responded.

His voice was more or less far away as he brooded on other matters—chiefly the atomic disintegration, which must be eating away the planet. Indeed, hardly had he answered the Amazon before there came a sudden tremendous concussion. It was some kind of deep explosion which set the around quivering with the incipiency of earthquake. The quartet looked about them from the airlock, startled. The little people, on the point of dispersing to hunt for more small animals underground, paused in sudden panic.

In the far distance the silver plain was marred by a sudden eruption of flame and molten metal spouting from the ground and reaching in clouds of yellow smoke to the cobalt sky.

"Volcanic eruption," Abna said grimly, staring at the disturbance. "That disintegrating fire must have touched off a volcanic seam from that molten crater underground, and this is the result. As we know, the heart of the planet is still in a fluid state— Hey, there!" he broke off, yelling. "You have no time to look for any more small animals. Too dangerous. Just bring what you have and grab what food you've got and come with us. We'll see you have a good supply and you'll have to figure the rest out for yourselves."

The people turned instantly and made a dash for the *Ultra*.

"Stand by," Abna said briefly, glancing over his shoulder. "We'll have to 'ration' it out as best we can."

Which was duly done. As Abna had calculated, 100 only could be permitted to crowd into the *Ultra*'s confines, most of them carrying odds and ends of possessions. The rest were held back, blank disappointment showing in their faces.

"We're going to have to act fast," Abna said worriedly, as the Amazon came to his side. "Four more trips to get them all away. We'll just have to dump this 100 and fly straight back nonstop.'"

The Amazon nodded slowly. "And food? What do you propose to do for them?"

"Only one thing I can do—supply them with several tons of synthetic food, and give them all the stimulants and fertilizers we've got, together with seeds for plants and food-crops."

"You know, I've just thought of something," Mexone mused. "Antara is presently devoid of animal and insect life, but the Tucans are bringing with them a number of small animals. They will almost certainly be carrying various parasites and all kinds of small organisms— maybe insects—on their coats and skins. In time—"

"Yes, quite possibly a whole new ecology will be created in time," the Amazon agreed impatiently. "But we haven't got time right now to mull over non-essential scientific issues. We've simply got to concentrate everything we have into getting to Antara, and then returning to Tuca as quickly as possible to ferry more people to safety!"

* * * * * *

The journey continued with ever-mounting speed, and Ekon, the interpreter, and his fellow men and women gazed out in silence on the wastes of the Milky Way, fascinated by the journey they were making. Abna drove the *Ultra* at the maximum speed possible for the Tucans to endure, and as the hours passed the rehabilitated planet of Antara gradually emerged from the depths as a planet of clouds, air, and water.

Swiftly Abna brought the huge machine to rest at the edge of one of the lakes, then he looked intently toward the newly created 'pasture' areas. Apparently the stimulating beams had done their work, for green plants were already flourishing in their hundreds.

Abna did not waste any time. He herded the 100 outside as fast as possible, then, with the Amazon, Viona and Mexone to help him, he unloaded several cases of synthetic food and seeds. The problem of drinking supplies was easily solved by reason of the nearby lake.

"All we can do for now," Abna said finally. "We've got to dash back—in fact, several times. Otherwise it will be too late."

He hurried back into the machine with the others and again started up the power plant. In a matter of seconds the *Ultra* was in the void again, and this time

Abna really put on the power, stepping up the velocity in order that the return trip could be made as fast as possible.

Flying through dense clouds of sulphuric smoke, using the tall silver pillar as a landmark, Abna finally brought the *Ultra* down close to its previous position, then he quickly opened the airlock and stood gazing outside. In the distance, dozens of the little people were advancing, shouting with joy at the return of their saviors.

Otherwise, the view was menacing. Clouds of sulphuric smoke were drifting heavily over the sky, blotting out the glare of the merciless sun. Down below the smoke, the people were running in their hundreds, some of them clasping what were obviously small animals in their arms.

"Evidently they risked getting a few more animals from underground," he said to the Amazon. "All to the good. They can breed and provide flesh food for them."

The Amazon nodded, too busy moving the little folk about to ensure maximum comfort to pay much attention to what Abna was saying.... Then again the power plant whirred with ever-increasing sound and the great machine shot like a bullet through the smoke and upper atmosphere into the void.

Abna made the landing on Antara without difficulty, stopping only long enough to herd the little folk into the welcoming midst of Ekon and the others. Then traveling at prodigious speed off again into the void.

The third and fourth 100 people were transported

without any visible sign of serious deterioration in Tuca's physical structure—but on the last journey for the final 100 there was a different story.... Somewhat weary, grim-eyed, the quartet surveyed the face of Tuea as they descended to it for the last time.

It had changed immeasurably. Hardly a portion of its surface was not pockmarked with devouring fire and volcanic eruption, and the air disturbances as the *Ultra* swept down made it bounce uncomfortably as though it were being thrown down gigantic steps.

Steering by instruments, so dense was the smoke, Abna finally succeeded in settling the vessel in the usual spot, then he leaned to the airlock and opened it. In silence he stood there, puzzled. There was no sign of the last 100 Tucans.

They were grimly silent for a moment, vile-smelling smoke curling about their nostrils, then suddenly Viona gave a cry.

"Look! Lava! A tidal wave of it—between us and the *Ultra*!"

She was right. The hazy spaces between the quartet and the *Ultra* cleared for a moment to reveal a two-foot high gray line pouring from a newly opened volcanic crater. The viscid, smoking substance moved forward irresistibly, dissolving the silver of the plain and coming slowly toward the settlement.

"Abna! The *Ultra*'s cut off!" The Amazon's voice was suddenly taut with anxiety. Before Abna could answer her there came a sudden tremendous explosion from the smoking ravine in the near distance. The four staggered with the earth-shock; then when they had steadied, they beheld yet another lava flood emerging, sweeping toward them in devouring fire.

"Fire both sides and heading towards us," Abna said grimly. "That isn't very pretty—" He glanced toward the only way out—to the higher ground—then shook his head. "That would only be postponing the end. Here! Up this pillar!"

"But what—" Viona started to say, but Abna cut her short.

"No time to argue. The immediate thing is to ensure our safety, if only temporarily. Up you get!"

Viona obeyed, shinning up the pillar with easy agility, until she reached the ledge fixed around the top. Then she paused and gently levered herself into a sitting position. Mexone followed her, then the Amazon, and finally Abna. They sat on the four sides of the pillar, gazing into the murk.

"Fortunate for us we have this praying ledge, or whatever it is," Abna remarked. "We can relax for a moment while we think what comes next."

"Look!" Mexone gasped suddenly. "Look at the *Ultra*!"

The others jerked their eyes to it in the smoky twilight. The lava flood had reached the monster space-ship and was lifting it, like a cork on water. Gradually the massive flyer was on the move, being carried away into the distance.

"How far do you think it will go?" Viona asked, staring hard.

"That we don't know," Abna replied. "The lava will carry it onwards. If there's more lava, it may be carried just anywhere. Even worse, it might fall into a chasm, be covered with molten metal, and lost. A dozen things can happen...."

Utterly helpless to rectify the situation, they were compelled to watch the vessel being carried away. Occasionally, smoke obscured it, and at each reappearance it was farther away. Presumably it would stop when at last the lava had spent itself.

To test the plasma below them, Abna lowered himself down the pillar. As he expected, it was a quagmire of molten metal. For some time nobody spoke.

"There's one thing puzzles me," Mexone remarked, after a while. "I've been meaning to mention it, but in the general excitement it slipped my memory.... Where have the waves of exhilaration gone? Remember how they were mainly responsible for keeping our spirits up? I don't recall feeling them since the first stage of the machine was dismantled down below."

CHAPTER NINE
ADRIFT IN SPACE

Abna considered. Then: "That was probably when they ceased. Must have been something in the first stage which caused them." He surveyed the smoke-ridden landscape. "There arises yet another danger, and the grimmest one of all. If this plasma doesn't cool very quickly, the real disintegration from below might beat it."

The others were silent for a moment as they weighed up the significance of the statement.

"Do you think the disintegration can come that quickly?" the Amazon asked.

"I can't think why not. The farther it spreads, the more rapid will be the chain reaction. It's an unpleasant thought to face—but there it is."

In spite of their physiques, the four began to feel a drowsy tiredness settling upon them.

"Three sleep and one stay awake," Abna said finally. "Tie yourselves slightly. It's the only way, I'll take first watch."

So, not very comfortably, fashioning the ropes after the style of crude hammocks, the Amazon, Viona, and Mexone prepared to rest—and to a certain extent succeeded. Abna still sat on, aware by now that the sun was setting behind the smoke pall. And presently night came.

Silent, Abna speculated somewhat morosely on these fiercely burning fires. The air stank of sulphur and volcanic discharge. It was warm and sultry, too, everything blanketed in by the dense cloudbanks. There was none of the rapid radiation from the surface, which was normal to the planet.

Abna mused on the vanished hundred. Plainly they must have walked into some kind of trap. It was a regrettable tragedy, but quite unavoidable. In any case, Abna had his own immediate predicament—and that of the others—to think of, and he did so deeply. So at length his four-hour watch came to an end and he shook the Amazon into wakefulness for her to take over. She did so in silence, so as not to disturb the soundly sleeping Viona and Mexone, and as it had been for Abna so it was for her. The hours passed in a silent survey of the volcanic fires smoldering dangerously in the dark.

Then she became aware of something else, far away in the distance. At first it was so illusive she thought it was her imagination—a thin line of violet flame extending from horizon to horizon. Not perhaps an illusion but a display of something akin to the auroral draperies, engendered by the interplay of electrical forces. It was not until the ground shook under a sudden tremor that the Amazon realized what it was. It was advancing disintegration, giving off that queer violet glow in which were encompassed many deadly radiations.

It was when the ground quaked again violently and there was a simultaneous whiplash of lightning and crack of thunder that she stirred and quickly awakened Abna.

"Disintegration on the way!" she said urgently, and he stirred out of slumber.

He watched the distant line of violet fire for a time and at last gave a grim nod.

"You're right, Vi—it's moved quicker than I expected. We've got to decide on what move we must make."

Viona and Mexone were quickly awakened and given the facts. In alarm they watched the distant line of violet light, then glanced overhead at the flashes of lightning preceding the disturbance.

"It's coming this way, and the rate it's going it won't take—"

Abna could not finish his sentence. The most violent earthquake shock to date suddenly broke in upon him. The landscape heaved and then seemed to slew around drunkenly. As things steadied again Anna said sharply:

"You realize what happened just then?"

"At a rough guess I'd say a chunk of the planet broke away," the Amazon replied. "That would cause the wild lurch, and the swinging was the restoration of balance to a new state of equilibrium."

"Right! The whole planet's breaking away like a piece of crumbly cake. We're lucky this pillar's still standing. I'm going down to see what state the plasma's in."

Thunder belched and lightning ripped vividly across the sky as Abna retied the rope about his waist. In a matter of seconds he was swinging down into the depths. To his surprise he had only a little way to go. The plasma had risen considerably in the dark hours and was again on the move, bubbling at times, and a good deal hotter than it had been formerly. Quickly he scrambled back to safety.

"Things are worse than I thought," he said, pulling the rope free. "The lava flow isn't much more than six feet below us, and on the move. Fortunately it isn't at a heat sufficient to melt this pillar, but escape is quite impossible. We'd be instantly burned to death...." He peered intently in the flashes of lightning. "All this won't do much good to the *Ultra*. It must be being carried farther and farther away, or it might even be buried in the stuff."

The Amazon was about to speak when a shattering roar exploded into the darkness. With it there came another wild swing of the planet. The silver column leaned slightly, and then stopped, leaving the four scrambling to restore their former equilibrium. Even as it was, they were on a slant, only keeping their feet with difficulty upon the tilted ledge. And not very far below them they could see and hear the deadly tide of molten matter flowing past.

"This is certainly the end of kingpin planet," Abna said breathlessly, straightening up.

"And the end of us if this column dips any more," Mexone added in alarm. "It's on a terrific tilt even as it is, and if it—"

Thunder drowned him out. Not a second later there arose a sudden stiff breeze. At an amazing speed it increased to a wind, and from a wind to a gale. Finally, it was a hurricane, flattening the four against the pillar with its ferocity.

"Joy added to joy!" Abna yelled. "And there's reason for this, too."

"Naturally," the Amazon shouted back. "But what is it?"

"The air is being sucked away by the collapse of the planet. It's being dragged out into the vacuum of outer space."

Such indeed was the case. With the general disintegration, the gravity of the planet was weakening—a fact of which the four were already aware—and with the weakening of the gravity, the atmosphere itself was no longer being held down in a stable manner. In the screaming vortex of the hurricane it was roaring into outer space, the heavier gases alone remaining.

And nearer the violet line which was crumbling a world into dust....

For a second or two after this latest upheaval there was comparative peace—if a hurricane and violent thunder could he called peace. But at least it gave the troubled four time to think.

"If we're not thrown into the lava or sucked into some volcanic maw, there's only one thing that can happen to us," Abna said. "We'll be sucked into space."

"Which means instant death," the Amazon said quietly.

"I do not agree, Vi—and as an excellent scientist, neither should you. Time and again we've proved that it is possible to survive in outer space for a short time—even have the power of movement. Especially so in our case because of our perfect physique."

The Amazon shrugged in the blaze of lightning. "Survive for a short time or otherwise, what's the use? The void's the void, and it will get us in the end."

"In space," Abna continued deliberately, "we do not explode if we first exhale all air from our lungs. There is, therefore, no pressure to blow us asunder. On the other hand, the void is a perfect insulator, so we retain our bodily warmth for a while—but only for a while—until the vacuum draws it out of us and we die. We suffocate from lack of air before we freeze. That we've proved over and again. If we are flung into free space our last hope is the *Ultra*. If it is flung free by the catastrophe, it will be floating in the void some-where nearest to the closest field of gravity. Somehow, if we get into the void, we must reach it! We all know how to undo the safety lock. That is our last chance. Understood?"

"Understood," the Amazon agreed.

With that, Abna became silent. The hurricane and storm were still raging, and the gravity had become noticeably less. In truth, about only half of the original planet remained, and that was rapidly collapsing as the galloping chain reaction progressed.

Thereafter the four lost track of time as they perched on their narrow ledge on the lopsided pillar, with the molten lava flowing not far below them. That thin violet line somehow had a hypnotic fascination for them. There was something uncanny about the way in which it destroyed everything in its tracks, coming ever nearer—and yet nearer.

By this time the *Ultra* must have been swept into space, since the region where it had last been seen was now behind the violet line—and behind the violet line was the ever-shortening horizon, which led into nothing. The raging air was filled with the curious fizzing tumult that seemed to be a characteristic of the disintegration.

The silver pillar lurched again, but it did not fall. What remained of the planet shifted to a new balance, with the inevitable accompanying earthquake. Lava and violet line heaved together and then settled again. Abna, hanging on to the ledge tightly, glanced at the others. He beheld three strained faces looking downward.

"The air's going fast," he shouted, as the vapors streamed past with hurricane force. "At this rate it will be gone before the pillar collapses."

There was no answer from the Amazon, Viona, or Mexone. They were too intent in concentrating on the immediate danger. For danger there certainly was, as the line of disintegration came closer.

There was still quite a deal of the planet left, and as

long as some mass remained, that mass had gravitation. If they were cast free into space as the disintegration caught up, they would inevitably be dragged back to the remains of the planet—and that meant to the lava field, which still existed below. This flow was now, however, cut off from its source, so there was no possibility of an increase.

The violet line of disintegration was now so close that the four could feel the battering violence of the ultraviolet waves it was giving off. Conscious of the danger, they dropped their purple goggles into place. Immediately their whole world was limited to a vision of a sparkling line of fire coming closer, and yet closer.

"One last instruction—" Abna said abruptly. "When we are thrown into space, as seems likely, use your proton guns as reactors to fire you away from the planet. You know how I mean—"

His words were abruptly cut off as atmosphere from this particular region whirled into nothing and was gone. Instantly the quartet exhaled, and thereafter it was a matter of lung control. They were aware of the pillar sliding downwards and at the same moment they leaped free of it, utilizing the weakened gravitation. This was quite the most amazing jump they had ever made. It carried them over the line of disintegration and into space itself. Beyond, there was no planet. Only the merciless, endless void.

With a quick movement Abna pulled off his goggles, and instantly the stars of space came into view. He glanced about him and saw the Amazon, Viona, and

Mexone floating outwards into infinity, while not very far below was the disintegrating world of Tuca.

Gradually, as the pull of what remained of the planet exerted itself, the quartet began to drift downwards, until Abna set the example by snatching out his gun and firing it between his feet.

Immediately the recoil action sent him shooting upward.... A brief glance satisfied him that the others were doing likewise.

But now there was the torture of airlessness to be combated, and a very real thing it was. That, and the relentless zero of space, were rapidly making inroads. There were only seconds to go if survival was to be possible.

Abna looked about him through blurred eyes, and almost at once he beheld the *Ultra*. By the law of mass and gravity it was lying close to the remains of the boiling, flaming, disintegrating planet. Abna pointed: the only signal he could make, and again firing his proton gun as his motive power he swept down toward the huge machine. The conditions were such that he was sure he would never make it—yet he did, because everything depended on it.

Choking in the airless vacuum, he clawed his way to the airlock—open exactly as it had been left. His senses fast deserting him, he held on until the Amazon, then Mexone, and last of all Viona, floundered in also. They dropped to the floor and remained still, blood trickling from their nostrils.

Every movement feeling as though it was weighed

down by countless tons, Abna battled his way with falling strength to the switchboard and snapped down three controls. One for the airlock to close, the second for the air pumps to start working, and the third for a weak current to start up the power plant.... Then unconsciousness crashed down upon him.

Seconds passed, then minutes. The trickle of current into the power plant remained, sufficient to drive the *Ultra* away from the collapsing remains of Tuca. And, as the air was slowly restored to their lungs the four began to recover. Abna was the first to return to consciousness and he staggered to his feet, aware of a violent tingling in sill parts of his body as circulation, slowed almost to zero by the vacuum of space, started up again.

One by one the others came to, and for all of them there was fifteen minutes of exquisite anguish as their bodies fought back to normal.

"Well, we made it!" Abna said finally. "Even if we did nearly kill ourselves doing it. By this time we must be quite a distance from both Antara and what remains of Tuca. I don't suppose there'd be any point in going back to Antara and telling them the details? They're safe to pursue their own way, and our job's done."

Viona smiled. "That's more like it. A chance to relax for a while."

"And after that?" the Amazon asked, raising an eyebrow. "You'll want something else. All of ns will."

"Don't worry," Abna chuckled. "You'll get it, if what I have in mind comes off."

"Now what's coming?"' asked Mexone uneasily.

"Only this." Abna patted the tiny camera still strapped to his instrument belt. "Remember the photographs I took of that wonder probability machine? Remember, too, that I was projected into the region of misplaced probabilities?"

"Yes." The Amazon nodded slowly. "We remember."

"A different space," Abna went on, with an other-world look in his eye. "Where love is hate, where up is down, where to progress is to reverse—a muddled, incredible state of affairs to our ordered senses, yet incredibly fascinating. The region where probability has not the ordered equilibrium it has here. The glimpse I had, and was forced to leave, has made me anxious to see more. Maybe even crusade."

"And so?" the Amazon asked, though she knew what was coming.

"I propose we find a deserted planet somewhere, build a new probability machine from the photographs I have in the camera, together with our memories, and so project ourselves into this unknown space. It is yet another facet of the lifelong duty to which we are dedicated. There is no telling what we may learn."

"No telling," the Amazon agreed, watching as Abna took the camera from his belt. "Where love is hate, where up is down, where perhaps knowledge is ignorance...."

"And ignorance, knowledge," Abna finished for her, and set the camera down purposefully on the central table.

ABOUT THE AUTHOR

British writer JOHN RUSSELL FEARN was born near Manchester, England, in 1908. As a child he devoured the science fiction of Wells and Verne, and was a voracious reader of the Boys' Story Papers. He was also fascinated by the cinema, and first broke into print in 1931 with a series of articles in *Film Weekly*.

He then quickly sold his first novel, *The Intelligence Gigantic*, to the American magazine, *Amazing Stories*. Over the next fifteen years, writing under several pseudonyms, Fearn became one of the most prolific contributors to all of the leading US science fiction pulps, including such legendary publications as *Astounding Stories*, *Startling Stories*, *Thrilling Wonder Stories*, and *Weird Tales*.

During the late 1940s he diversified into writing novels for the UK market, and also created his famous superwoman character, The Golden Amazon, for the prestigious Canadian magazine, the Toronto *Star Weekly*. In the early 1950s in the UK, his fifty-two novels as "Vargo Statten" were bestsellers, most notably his novelization of the film, *Creature from the Black Lagoon*.

Apart from science fiction, he had equal success with westerns, romances, and detective fiction, writing an amazing total of 180 novels—most of them in a period of just ten years—before his early death in 1960. His work has been translated into nine languages, and continues to be reprinted and read worldwide.